30.09.2014
14.10.2014
1/2/17.
3/1

Please renew or return items by the date
shown on your receipt

www.hertsdirect.org/libraries

Renewals and enquiries: 0300 123 4049
Textphone for hearing or 0300 123 4041
speech impaired users:

L32

MARK TWAIN

AMERICAN DROLLERIES

SELECTED STORIES

DAUNT BOOKS

This edition first published in 2011 by
Daunt Books
83 Marylebone High Street
London W1U 4QW

1

A CIP catalogue record for this title is
available from the British Library.

ISBN 978 1 907970 04 7

Typeset by Antony Gray
Illustrations © Alys Jones
Printed and bound by
T J International Ltd, Padstow, Cornwall
www.dauntbooks.co.uk

Contents

Cannibalism in the Cars

I visited St Louis lately, and on my way west, after changing cars at Terre Haute, Indiana, a mild, benevolent-looking gentleman of about forty-five, or maybe fifty, came in at one of the way-stations and sat down beside me. We talked together pleasantly on various subjects for an hour, perhaps, and I found him exceedingly intelligent and entertaining. When he learned that I was from Washington, he immediately began to ask questions about various public men, and about Congressional affairs; and I saw very shortly that I was conversing with a man who was perfectly familiar with the ins and outs of political life at the Capital, even to the ways and manners, and customs of procedure of Senators and Representatives in the Chambers of the National Legislature.

Presently two men halted near us for a single moment, and one said to the other: 'Harris, if you'll do that for me, I'll never forget you, my boy.'

My new comrade's eyes lighted pleasantly. The words had touched upon a happy memory, I thought. Then his face settled into thoughtfulness – almost into gloom. He turned to me and said, 'Let me tell you a story; let me give you a secret chapter of my life – a chapter that has never been referred to by me since its events transpired. Listen patiently, and promise that you will not interrupt me.'

I said I would not, and he related the following strange adventure, speaking sometimes with animation, sometimes with melancholy, but always with feeling and earnestness.

THE STRANGER'S NARRATIVE

On the 19th December, 1853, I started from St Louis in the evening train, bound for Chicago. There were only twenty-four passengers, all told. There were no ladies and no children. We were in excellent spirits, and pleasant acquaintanceships were soon formed. The journey bade fair to be a happy one, and no individual in the party, I think, had even the vaguest presentiment of the horrors we were soon to undergo. At 11 p.m. it began to snow hard. Shortly after leaving the small village of Weldon, we entered upon that tremendous prairie solitude that stretches its leagues on leagues of houseless dreariness far away towards the Jubilee Settlements. The winds unobstructed by trees or hills, or even vagrant rocks, whistled fiercely across the level desert, driving the falling snow before it like spray from the crested waves of a stormy sea. The snow was deepening fast, and we knew, by the diminished speed of the train, that the engine was ploughing through it with steadily increasing difficulty. Indeed it almost came to a dead halt sometimes, in the midst of great drifts that piled themselves like colossal graves across the track. Conversation began to flag. Cheerfulness gave place to grave concern. The possibility of being imprisoned in the snow, on the bleak prairie, fifty miles from any house, presented itself to every mind, and extended its depressing influence over every spirit.

At two o'clock in the morning I was aroused out of an uneasy slumber by the ceasing of all motion about me. The appalling truth flashed upon me instantly – we were captives in a snow-drift! 'All hands to the rescue!' Every man sprang to obey. Out into the wild night, the pitchy darkness, the billowing snow, the driving storm, every soul leaped, with the consciousness that a moment lost now might bring destruction to us all. Shovels, hands, boards – anything, everything that could displace snow, was brought into instant requisition. It was a weird picture, that small company of frantic men fighting the banking snows, half in the blackest shadow and half in the angry light of the locomotive's reflector.

One short hour sufficed to prove the utter uselessness of our efforts. The storm barricaded the track with a dozen drifts while we dug one away. And worse than this, it was discovered that the last grand charge the engine had made upon the enemy had broken the fore-and-aft shaft of the driving-wheel! With a free track before us we should still have been helpless. We entered the car wearied with labour, and very sorrowful. We gathered about the stoves, and gravely canvassed our situation. We had no provisions whatever – in this lay our chief distress. We could not freeze, for there was a good supply of wood in the tender. This was our only comfort. The discussion ended at last in accepting the disheartening decision of the conductor – viz.: That it would be death for any man to attempt to travel fifty miles on foot through snow like that. We could not send for help, and even if we could, it could not come. We must submit and await, as patiently as we might, succour or starvation! I think the stoutest heart there felt a momentary chill when those words were uttered.

Within the hour conversation subsided to a low murmur here and there about the car, caught fitfully between the rising and falling of the blast; the lamps grew dim; and the majority of the castaways settled themselves among the flickering shadows to think – to forget the present if they could – to sleep, if they might.

The eternal night – it surely seemed eternal to us – wore its lagging hours away at last, and the cold grey dawn broke in the east. As the light grew stronger the passengers began to stir and give signs of life, one after another, and each in turn pushed his slouched hat up from his forehead, stretched his stiffened limbs, and glanced out at the windows upon the cheerless prospect. It was cheerless indeed! – not a living thing visible anywhere, not a human habitation; nothing but a vast white desert; uplifted sheets of snow drifting hither and thither before the wind – a world of eddying flakes shutting out the firmament above.

All day we moped about the cars, saying little, thinking much. Another lingering, dreary night – and hunger.

Another dawning – another day of silence, sadness, wasting hunger, hopeless watching for succour that could not come. A night of restless slumber, filled with dreams of feasting – wakings distressed with the gnawings of hunger.

The fourth day came and went – and the fifth! Five days of dreadful imprisonment! A savage hunger looked out at every eye. There was in it a sign of awful import – the foreshadowing of a something that was vaguely shaping itself in every head – a something which no tongue dared yet to frame into words.

The sixth day passed – the seventh dawned upon as gaunt and haggard and hopeless a company of men as ever stood in the shadow of death. It must out now! That thing which had been growing up in every heart was ready to leap from every lip at last! Nature had been taxed to the utmost – she must yield. RICHARD H. GASTON, of Minnesota, tall, cadaverous, and pale, rose up. All knew what was coming. All prepared – every emotion, every semblance of excitement was smothered – only a calm, thoughtful seriousness appeared in the eyes that were lately so wild.

'Gentlemen – It cannot be delayed longer! The time is at hand! We must determine which of us shall die to furnish food for the rest!'

MR JOHN J. WILLIAMS, of Illinois, rose and said: 'Gentlemen – I nominate the Rev James Sawyer, of Tennessee.'

MR WM. R. ADAMS, of Indiana, said: 'I nominate Mr Daniel Slate, of New York.'

MR CHARLES J. LANGDON: 'I nominate Mr Samuel A. Bowen, of St. Louis.'

MR SLOTE: 'Gentlemen – I desire to decline in favour of Mr John A. Van Nostrand, Jr., of New Jersey.'

MR GASTON: 'If there be no objection, the gentleman's desire will be acceded to.'

MR VAN NOSTRAND objecting, the resignation of Mr Slote was rejected. The resignations of Messrs Sawyer and Bowen were also offered, and refused upon the same grounds.

MR A. L. BASCOM, of Ohio: 'I move that the nominations now close, and that the House proceed to an election by ballot.'

MR SAWYER: 'Gentlemen – I protest earnestly against these proceedings. They are, in every way, irregular and unbecoming. I must beg to move that they be dropped at once, and that we elect a chairman of the meeting and proper officers to assist him, and then we can go on with the business before us understandingly.'

MR BELKNAP, of Iowa: 'Gentlemen – I object. This is no time to stand upon forms and ceremonious observances.

For more than seven days we have been without food. Every moment we lose in idle discussion increases our distress. I am satisfied with the nominations that have been made – every gentleman present is, I believe – and I, for one, do not see why we should not proceed at once to elect one or more of them. I wish to offer a resolution—'

Mr GASTON: 'It would be objected to, and have to lie over one day under the rules, thus bringing about the very delay you wish to avoid. The gentleman from New Jersey—'

Mr VAN NOSTRAND: 'Gentlemen, I am a stranger among you; I have not sought the distinction that has been conferred upon me, and I feel a delicacy.'

Mr MORGAN, of Alabama: 'I move the previous question.'

The motion was carried, and further debate shut off, of course. The motion to elect officers was passed, and under it Mr Gaston was chosen Chairman, Mr Blake, Secretary, Messrs Holcomb, Dyer, and Baldwin, a Committee on nominations, and Mr R. M. Howland, Purveyor, to assist the committee in making selections.

A recess of half an hour was then taken, and some little caucusing followed. At the sound of the gavel the meeting reassembled, and the committee reported in favour of Messrs George Ferguson, of Kentucky, Lucien Hermann, of Louisiana, and W. Messick, of Colorado, as candidates. The report was accepted.

Mr ROGERS, of Missouri: 'Mr President – The report being properly before the House now, I move to amend it by substituting for the name of Mr Hermann that of Mr Lucius Harris, of St Louis, who is well and honourably known to us all. I do not wish to be understood as casting the least reflection upon the high character and standing of the gentleman from Louisiana – far from it. I respect and esteem him as much as any gentleman here present possibly can; but none of us can be blind to the fact that he has lost more flesh during the week that we have lain here than any among you – none of us can be blind to the fact that the committee has been derelict in its duty, either through negligence or a graver fault, in thus offering for our suffrages a gentleman who, however pure his own motives may be, has really less nutriment in him—'

THE CHAIR: 'The gentleman from Missouri will take his seat. The Chair cannot allow the integrity of the Committee to be questioned save by the regular course, under the rules. What action will the House take upon the gentleman's motion?'

MR HALLIDAY, of Virginia: 'I move to further amend the report by substituting Mr Harvey Davis, of Oregon, for Mr Messick. It may be urged by gentlemen that the hardships and privations of a frontier life have rendered Mr Davis tough; but, gentlemen, is this a time to cavil at toughness? is this a time to be fastidious concerning trifles? is this a time to dispute about matters of paltry significance? No, gentlemen, bulk is what we desire – substance, weight, bulk – these are the supreme requisites now – not talent, not genius, not education. I insist upon my motion.'

MR MORGAN (excitedly): 'Mr Chairman – I do most strenuously object to this amendment. The gentleman from Oregon is old, and furthermore, is bulky only in bone – not in flesh. I ask the gentleman from Virginia if it is soup we want instead of solid sustenance? if he would delude us with shadows? if he would mock our suffering with an Oregonian spectre? I ask him if he can look upon the anxious faces around him, if he can gaze into our sad eyes, if he can listen to the beating of our expectant hearts, and still thrust this famine-stricken fraud upon us? I ask him if he can think of our desolate state, of our past sorrows, of our dark furore, and still unpityingly foist upon us this wreck, this ruin, this tottering swindle, this gnarled and blighted and sapless vagabond from Oregon's inhospitable shores? Never!' (Applause.)

The amendment was put to vote, after a fiery debate, and lost. Mr Harris was substituted on the first amendment. The balloting then began. Five ballots were held without a choice. On the sixth, Mr Harris was elected, all voting for him but himself. It was then moved that his election should be ratified by acclamation, which was lost, in consequence of his again voting against himself.

Mr Radway moved that the House now take up the remaining candidates, and go into an election for breakfast. This was carried.

On the first ballot there was a tie, half the members favouring one candidate on account of his youth, and half favouring the other on account of his superior size. The President gave the casting vote for the latter, Mr Messick. This decision created considerable dissatisfaction among the friends of Mr Ferguson, the defeated candidate, and there was some talk of demanding a new ballot; but in the midst of it, a motion to adjourn was carried, and the meeting broke up at once.

The preparations for supper diverted the attention of the Ferguson faction from the discussion of their grievance for a long time, and then, when they would have taken it up again, the happy announcement that Mr Harris was ready, drove all thought of it to the winds.

We improvised tables by propping up the backs of car-seats, and sat down with hearts full of gratitude to the finest supper that had blessed our vision for seven torturing days. How changed we were from what we had been a few short hours before! Hopeless, sad-eyed misery, hunger, feverish anxiety, desperation, then – thankfulness, serenity, joy too deep for utterance now. That I know was the cheeriest hour of my eventful life. The wind howled, and blew the snow wildly about our prison-house, but they were powerless to distress us anymore. I liked Harris. He might have been better done, perhaps, but I am free to say that no man ever agreed with me better than Harris, or afforded me so large a degree of satisfaction. Messick was very well, though rather high-flavoured, but for genuine nutritiousness and delicacy of fibre, give me Harris. Messick had his good points – I will not attempt to deny it, nor do I wish to do it – but he was no more fitted for breakfast than a mummy would be, sir – not a bit. Lean? – why, bless me! – and tough? Ah, he was very tough! You could not imagine it – you could never imagine anything like it.

'Do you mean to tell me that—'

Do not interrupt me, please. After breakfast we elected a man by the name of Walker, from Detroit, for supper. He was very good. I wrote his wife so afterwards. He was worthy of all praise. I shall always remember Walker. He was a little rare, but very good. And then the next morning we had Morgan, of Alabama, for breakfast. He was one of the finest men I ever sat down to – handsome, educated, refined, spoke several languages fluently – a perfect gentle-man – he was a perfect gentleman, and singularly juicy. For supper we had that Oregon patriarch, and he *was* a fraud, there is no question about it – old, scraggy, tough – nobody can picture the reality. I finally said, gentlemen, you can do as you like, but *I* will wait for another election.

And Grimes, of Illinois, said, 'Gentlemen, *I* will wait also. When you elect a man that has *something* to recommend him, I shall be glad to join you again.' It soon became evident that there was general dissatisfaction with Davis, of Oregon, and so, to preserve the goodwill that had prevailed so pleasantly since we had had Harris, an election was called, and the result of it was that Baker, of Georgia, was chosen. He was splendid! Well, well – after that we had Doolittle, and Hawkins, and McElroy (there was some complaint about McElroy, because he was uncommonly short and thin), and Penrod, and two Smiths, and Bailey (Bailey had a wooden leg, which was clear loss, but he was otherwise good), and an Indian boy, and an organ-grinder, and a gentleman by the name of Buckminster – a poor stick of a vagabond that wasn't any good for company and no account for breakfast. We were glad we got him elected before relief came.

'And so the blessed relief *did* come at last?'

Yes, it came one bright sunny morning, just after election. John Murphy was the choice, and there never was a better, I am willing to testify; but John Murphy came home with us, in the train that came to succour us, and lived to marry the widow Harris—

'Relict of—'

Relict of our first choice. He married her, and is happy and respected and prosperous yet. Ah, it was like a novel, sir – it was like a romance. This is my stopping-place, sir; I must bid you goodbye. Anytime that you can make it convenient to tarry a day or two with me, I shall be glad to have you. I like you, sir; I have conceived an affection for you. I could like you as well as I liked Harris himself, sir. Good day, sir, and a pleasant journey.

He was gone. I never felt so stunned, so distressed, so bewildered in my life. But in my soul I was glad he was gone. With all his gentleness of manner and his soft voice, I shuddered whenever he turned his hungry eye upon me, and when I heard that I had achieved his perilous affection, and that I stood almost with the late Harris in his esteem, my heart fairly stood still!

I was bewildered beyond description. I did not doubt his word; I could not question a single item in a statement so stamped with the earnestness of truth as his; but its dreadful details overpowered me, and threw my thoughts into hopeless confusion.

I saw the conductor looking at me. I said, 'Who is that man?'

'He was a member of Congress once, and a good one. But he got caught in a snowdrift in the cars, and like to been starved to death. He got so frostbitten and frozen up generally, and used up for want of something to eat, that he was sick and out of his head two or three months afterwards. He is all right now, only he is a monomaniac, and when he gets on that old subject he never stops till he has eat up that whole carload of people he talks about. He would have finished the crowd by this time, only he had to get out here. He has got their names as pat as ABC. When he gets them all eat up but himself, he always says: "Then the hour for the usual election for breakfast having arrived, and there being no opposition, I was duly elected, after which, there being no objections offered, I resigned. Thus I am here." '

I felt inexpressibly relieved to know that I had only been listening to the harmless vagaries of a madman, instead of the genuine experiences of a bloodthirsty cannibal.

Jim Smiley and his Jumping Frog

Mr A. Ward,

DEAR SIR: – Well, I called on good-natured, garrulous old Simon Wheeler, and I inquired after your friend Leonidas W. Smiley, as you requested me to do, and I hereunto append the result. If you can get any information out of it you are cordially welcome to it. I have a lurking suspicion that your Leonidas W. Smiley is a myth – that you never knew such a personage, and that you only conjectured that if I asked old Wheeler about him it would remind him of his infamous Jim Smiley, and he would go to work and bore me nearly to death with some infernal reminiscence of him as long and tedious as it should be useless to me. If that was your design, Mr Ward, it will gratify you to know that it succeeded.

I found Simon Wheeler dozing comfortably by the barroom stove of the little old dilapidated tavern in the ancient mining camp of Boomerang, and I noticed that he was fat and bald-headed, and had an expression of winning gentleness and simplicity upon his tranquil countenance. He roused up and gave me good-day. I told him a friend of mine had commissioned me to make some inquiries about a cherished companion of his boyhood named Leonidas

W. Smiley – Rev Leonidas W. Smiley – a young minister of the gospel, who he had heard was at one time a resident of this village of Boomerang. I added that if Mr Wheeler could tell me anything about this Rev Leonidas W. Smiley, I would feel under many obligations to him.

Simon Wheeler backed me into a corner and blockaded me there with his chair – and then sat down and reeled off the monotonous narrative which follows this paragraph. He never smiled, he never frowned, he never changed his voice from the quiet, gently-flowing key to which he tuned the initial sentence, he never betrayed the slightest suspicion of enthusiasm – but all through the interminable narrative there ran a vein of impressive earnestness and sincerity, which showed me plainly that so far from his imagining that there was anything ridiculous or funny about his story, he regarded it as a really important matter, and admired its two heroes as men of transcendent genius in finesse. To me, the spectacle of a man drifting serenely along through such a queer yarn without ever smiling was exquisitely absurd. As I said before, I asked him to tell me what he knew of Rev Leonidas W. Smiley, and he replied as follows. I let him go on in his own way, and never interrupted him once.

*   *   *

There was a feller here once by the name of *Jim* Smiley, in the winter of '49 – or maybe it was the spring of '50 – I don't recollect exactly, somehow, though what makes me think it was one or the other is because I remember the big flume wasn't finished when he first come to the camp; but anyway, he was the curiousest man about always betting on anything that turned up you ever see, if he could get anybody to bet on the other side, and if he couldn't he'd change sides – any way that suited the other man would suit *him* – any way just so's *he* got a bet, he was satisfied. But still, he was lucky – uncommon lucky; he most always come out winner. He was always ready and laying for a chance; there couldn't be no solitary thing mentioned but what that feller'd offer to bet on it – and take any side you please, as I was just telling you: if there was a horse race, you'd find him flush or you find him busted at the end of it; if there was a dogfight, he'd bet on it; if there was a cat-fight, he'd bet on it; if there was a chickenfight, he'd bet on it; why if there was two birds setting on a fence, he would bet you which one would fly first – or if there was a camp meeting he would be there reglar to bet on parson Walker, which he judged to be the best exhorter about here, and so he was, too, and a good man; if he even see a straddle-bug start to go anywheres, he would bet you how long it would take him to get wherever he was going to, and if you took him up he would foller that straddle-bug to Mexico but what he would find out where he was bound for and how long he was on the road. Lots of the boys here has seen that Smiley and can tell you about him. Why, it never made no difference to *him* – he would bet on *anything* – the dangdest feller. Parson Walker's wife laid very sick, once, for a good while, and it seemed as if they warn't going to save her; but one morning he come in and Smiley asked him how she was, and he said she was considerable better – thank the Lord for his inf'nit mercy – and coming on so smart that with the blessing of Providence she'd get well yet – and Smiley, before he thought, says, 'Well, I'll resk two and a half that she don't anyway.'

Thish-yer Smiley had a mare – the boys called her the

fifteen-minute nag, but that was only in fu
because, of course, she was faster than that – a
win money on that horse, for all she was so slo
had the asthma, or the distemper, or the con
something of that kind. They used to give her two or three
hundred yards' start, and then pass her under way; but
always at the fag-end of the race she'd get excited and
desperate-like, and come cavorting and spraddling up, and
scattering her legs around limber, sometimes in the air, and
sometimes out to one side amongst the fences, and kicking
up m–o–r–e dust, and raising m–o–r–e racket with her
coughing and sneezing and blowing her nose – and always
fetch up at the stand just about a neck ahead, as near as you
could cipher it down.

And he had a little small bull-pup, that to look at him
you'd think he warn't worth a cent, but to set around and
look ornery, and lay for a chance to steal something. But
as soon as money was up on him he was a different dog –
his under-jaw'd begin to stick out like the for'castle of a
steamboat, and his teeth would uncover, and shine savage
like the furnaces. And a dog might tackle him, and bully-
rag him, and bite him, and throw him over his shoulder
two or three times, and Andrew Jackson – which was the
name of the pup – Andrew Jackson would never let on but
what he was satisfied, and hadn't expected nothing else –
and the bets being doubled and doubled on the other side
all the time, till the money was all up – and then all of a
sudden he would grab that other dog just by the joint of his
hind legs and freeze to it – not chaw, you understand, but
only just grip and hang on till they throwed up the sponge,
if it was a year. Smiley always came out winner on that pup
till he harnessed a dog once that didn't have no hind legs,

ecause they'd been sawed off in a circular saw, and when the thing had gone along far enough, and the money was all up, and he came to make a snatch for his pet holt, he saw in a minute how he'd been imposed on, and how the other dog had him in the door, so to speak, and he 'peared surprised, and then he looked sorter discouraged like, and didn't try no more to win the fight, and so he got shucked out bad. He gave Smiley a look as much as to say his heart was broke, and it was *his* fault, for putting up a dog that hadn't no hind legs for him to take holt of, which was his main dependence in a fight, and then he limped off a piece, and laid down and died. It was a good pup, was that Andrew Jackson, and would have made a name for hisself if he'd lived, for the stuff was in him, and he had genius – I know it, because he hadn't had no opportunities to speak of, and it don't stand to reason that a dog could make such a fight as he could under them circumstances, if he hadn't no talent. It always makes me feel sorry when I think of that last fight of his'on, and the way it turned out.

Well, thish-yer Smiley had rat-terriers and chicken cocks, and tomcats, and all them kind of things, till you couldn't rest, and you couldn't fetch nothing for him to bet on but he'd match you. He ketched a frog one day and took him home and said he cal'lated to educate him; and so he never done nothing for three months but set in his back yard and learn that frog to jump. And you bet you he *did* learn him, too. He'd give him a little hunch behind, and the next minute you'd see that frog whirling in the air like a doughnut – see him turn one summerset, or maybe a couple, if he got a good start, and come down flat-footed and all right, like a cat. He got him up so in the matter of ketching flies, and kept him in practice so constant, that he'd nail a fly every time as far as he could see him. Smiley said all a frog wanted was education, and he could do most anything – and I believe him. Why, I've seen him set Dan'l Webster down here on this floor – Dan'l Webster was the name of the frog – and sing out, 'Flies! Dan'l, flies,' and quicker'n you could wink, he'd spring straight up, and snake a fly off'n the counter there, and flop down on the floor again as solid as a gob of mud, and fall to scratching the side of his head with his hind foot as indifferent as if he hadn't no idea he'd done any more'n any frog might do. You never see a frog so modest and straightfor'ard as he was, for all he was so gifted. And when it come to fair-and-square jumping on a dead level, he could get over more ground at one straddle than any animal of his breed you ever see. Jumping on a dead level was his strong suit, you understand, and when it come to that, Smiley would ante up money on him as long as he had a red. Smiley was monstrous proud of his frog, and well he might be, for fellers that had travelled and ben everywheres all said he laid over any frog that ever *they* see.

Well, Smiley kept the beast in a little lattice box, and he used to fetch him downtown sometimes and lay for a bet.

One day a feller – a stranger in the camp, he was – come across him with his box, and says: 'What might it be that you've got in the box?'

And Smiley says, sorter indifferent like, 'It might be a parrot, or it might be a canary, maybe, but it ain't – it's only just a frog.'

And the feller took it, and looked at it careful, and turned it round this way and that, and says, 'H'm – so 'tis. Well, what's *he* good for?'

'Well,' Smiley says, easy and careless, 'He's good enough

for *one* thing I should judge – he can out-jump any frog in Calaveras county.'

The feller took the box again, and took another long, particular look, and give it back to Smiley and says, very deliberate, 'Well – I don't see no points about that frog that's any better'n any other frog.'

'Maybe you don't,' Smiley says. 'Maybe you understand frogs, and maybe you don't understand 'em; maybe you've had experience, and maybe you ain't only a amature, as it were. Anyways, I've got *my* opinion, and I'll resk forty dollars that he can out-jump any frog in Calaveras county.'

And the feller studied a minute, and then says, kinder sad, like, 'Well – I'm only a stranger here, and I ain't got no frog – but if I had a frog I'd bet you.'

And then Smiley says, 'That's all right – that's all right – if you'll hold my box a minute I'll go and get you a frog;' and so the feller took the box, and put up his forty dollars along with Smiley's, and set down to wait.

So he set there a good while thinking and thinking to hisself, and then he got the frog out and prized his mouth open and took a teaspoon and filled him full of quail-shot – filled him pretty near up to his chin – and set him on the floor. Smiley he went out to the swamp and slopped around in the mud for a long time, and finally he ketched a frog and fetched him in and give him to this feller and says:

'Now if you're ready, set him alongside of Dan'l, with his forepaws just even with Dan'l's, and I'll give the word.' Then he says, 'one – two – three – jump!' and him and the feller touched up the frogs from behind, and the new frog hopped off lively, but Dan'l give a heave, and hysted up his shoulders – so – like a Frenchman, but it wasn't no use – he couldn't budge; he was planted as solid as a anvil, and he couldn't no more stir than if he was anchored out. Smiley was a good deal surprised, and he was disgusted too, but he didn't have no idea what the matter was, of course.

The feller took the money and started away, and when he was going out at the door he sorter jerked his thumb over his shoulder – this way – at Dan'l, and says again, very deliberate, 'Well – *I* don't see no points about that frog that's any better'n any other frog.'

Smiley he stood scratching his head and looking down at Dan'l a long time, and at last he says, 'I do wonder what in the nation that frog throwed off for – I wonder if there ain't something the matter with him – he 'pears to look might baggy, somehow' – and he ketched Dan'l by the nap of the neck, and lifted him up and says, 'Why blame my cats if he don't weigh five pound' – and turned him upside down, and he belched out about a double-handful of shot. And then he see how it was, and he was the maddest man – he set the frog down and took out after that feller, but he never ketched him. And—

[Here Simon Wheeler heard his name called from the front yard, and got up to go and see what was wanted.] And turning to me as he moved away, he said: 'Just sit where you are, stranger, and rest easy – I ain't going to be gone a second.'

But by your leave, I did not think that a continuation of the history of the enterprising vagabond Jim Smiley would be likely to afford me much information concerning the Rev Leonidas W. Smiley, and so I started away.

At the door I met the sociable Wheeler returning, and he buttonholed me and recommenced: 'Well, thish-yer Smiley had a yaller one-eyed cow that didn't have no tail only just a short stump like a bannanner, and—'

'O, curse Smiley and his afflicted cow!' I muttered, good-naturedly, and bidding the old gentleman good-day, I departed.

Yours, truly,

MARK TWAIN

The Story of the Bad Little Boy
Who Didn't Come to Grief

Once there was a bad little boy, whose name was Jim – though, if you will notice, you will find that bad little boys are nearly always called James in your Sunday-school books. It was very strange, but still it was true, that this one was called Jim.

He didn't have any sick mother, either – a sick mother who was pious and had the consumption, and would be glad to lie down in the grave and be at rest, but for the strong love she bore her boy, and the anxiety she felt that the world would be harsh and cold towards him when she was gone. Most bad boys in the Sunday books are named James, and have sick mothers, who teach them to say, 'Now I lay me down,' etc., and sing them to sleep with sweet plaintive voices, and then kiss them goodnight, and kneel down by the bedside and weep. But it was different with this fellow. He was named Jim, and there wasn't anything the matter with his mother – no consumption, nor anything of that kind. She was rather stout than otherwise, and she was not pious; moreover, she was not anxious on Jim's account. She said if he were to break his neck, it wouldn't be much loss. She always spanked Jim to sleep, and she never kissed him goodnight; on the contrary, she boxed his ears when she was ready to leave him.

Once this little bad boy stole the key of the pantry and slipped in there and helped himself to some jam, and filled up the vessel with tar, so that his mother would never know the difference; but all at once a terrible feeling didn't come over him, and something didn't seem to whisper to him, 'Is it right to disobey my mother? Isn't it sinful to do this? Where do bad little boys go who gobble up their good kind mother's jam?' and then he didn't kneel down all alone and promise never to be wicked anymore, and rise up with a light, happy heart, and go and tell his mother all about it, and beg her forgiveness, and be blessed by her with tears of pride and thankfulness in her eyes. No; that is the way with all other bad boys in the books; but it happened otherwise with this Jim, strangely enough. He ate that jam, and said it was bully, in his sinful, vulgar way; and he put in the tar, and said that was bully also, and laughed, and observed that 'the old woman would get up and snort' when she found it out; and when she did find it out, he denied knowing anything about it, and she whipped him severely, and he did the crying himself. Everything about this boy was curious – everything turned out differently with him from the way it does to the bad Jameses in the books.

Once he climbed up in Farmer Acorn's apple-tree to steal apples, and the limb didn't break, and he didn't fall and break his arm, and get torn by the farmer's great dog, and then languish on a sickbed for weeks, and repent and become good. Oh! no; he stole as many apples as he wanted, and came down all right; and he was all ready for the dog, too, and knocked him endways with a brick when he came to tear him. It was very strange – nothing like it ever happened in those mild little books with marbled backs, and with pictures in them of men with swallow-tailed coats, and bell-crowned hats, and pantaloons that are short in the legs, and women with the waists of their dresses under their arms and no hoops on. Nothing like it in any of the Sunday-school books.

Once he stole the teacher's penknife, and when he was afraid it would be found out, and he would get whipped, he slipped it into George Wilson's cap – poor Widow Wilson's son, the moral boy, the good little boy of the village, who always obeyed his mother, and never told an untruth, and was fond of his lessons and infatuated with Sunday-school. And when the knife dropped from the cap, and poor George hung his head and blushed, as if in conscious guilt, and the grieved teacher charged the theft upon him, and was just in the very act of bringing the switch down upon his trembling shoulders, a white-haired improbable justice of the peace did not suddenly appear in their midst and strike an attitude and say, 'spare this noble boy – there stands the cowering culprit! I was passing the school-door at recess, and, unseen myself, I saw the theft committed!' And then Jim didn't get whaled, and the venerable justice didn't read the tearful school a homily, and take George by the hand and say such a boy deserved to be exalted, and then tell him to come and make his home with him, and sweep out the office, and make fires, and run errands, and chop wood, and study law, and help his wife do household labours, and have all the balance of the time to play, and get forty cents a month, and be happy. No; it would have happened that way in the books, but it didn't happen that way to Jim. No meddling old clam of a justice dropped in to make trouble, and so the model boy George got thrashed, and Jim was glad of it; because, you know, Jim hated moral boys. Jim said he was 'down on them milksops.' Such was the coarse language of this bad, neglected boy.

But the strangest thing that ever happened to Jim was the time he went boating on Sunday and didn't get drowned, and that other time that he got caught out in the storm when he was fishing on Sunday, and didn't get struck by lightning. Why, you might look, and look, all through the Sunday-school books, from now till next Christmas and you would never come across anything like this. Oh! no; you would find that all the bad boys who go boating on Sunday invariably get drowned; and all the bad boys who get caught out in storms, when they are fishing on Sunday, infallibly get struck by lightning. Boats with bad boys in them always upset on Sunday, and it always storms when bad boys go fishing on the Sabbath. How this Jim ever escaped is a mystery to me.

This Jim bore a charmed life – that must have been the way of it. Nothing could hurt him. He even gave the elephant in the menagerie a plug of tobacco, and the elephant didn't knock the top of his head off with his trunk. He browsed around the cupboard after essence of peppermint, and didn't make a mistake and drink aqua fortis. He stole his father's gun and went hunting on the Sabbath, and didn't shoot three or four of his fingers off. He struck his little sister on the temple with his fist when he was angry, and she didn't linger in pain through long summer days, and die with sweet words of forgiveness upon her lips that redoubled the anguish of his breaking heart. No; she got over it. He ran off and went to sea at last, and didn't come back and find himself sad and alone in the world, his loved ones sleeping in the quiet churchyard, and the vine-embowered home of his boyhood rumbled down and gone to decay. Ah! no he came home drunk as a piper, and got into the station house the first thing.

And he grew up, and married, and raised a large family, and brained them all with an axe one night, and got wealthy by all manner of cheating and rascality, and now he is the infernalest wickedest scoundrel in his native village, and is universally respected, and belongs to the Legislature.

So you see there never was a bad James in the Sunday-school books that had such a streak of luck as this sinful Jim with the charmed life.

The Story of the Good Little Boy Who Did Not Prosper

[The following has been written at the insistence of several literary friends, who thought that if the history of 'The Bad Little Boy Who Didn't Come to Grief' (a moral sketch which I published five or six years ago) was worthy of preservation several weeks in print, a fair and unprejudiced companion piece to it would deserve a similar immortality.

EDITORIAL MEMORANDUM]

Once there was a good little boy by the name of Jacob Blivens. He always obeyed his parents, no matter how absurd and unreasonable their demands were; and he always learned his book, and never was late at Sabbath school. He would not play hookey, even when his sober judgment told him it was the most profitable thing he could do. None of the other boys could ever make that boy out, he acted so strangely. He wouldn't lie, no matter how convenient it was. He just said it was wrong to lie, and that was sufficient for him. And he was so honest that he was simply ridiculous. The curious ways that that Jacob had surpassed everything. He wouldn't play marbles on Sunday, he wouldn't rob birds' nests, he wouldn't give hot pennies to organ-grinders' monkeys; he didn't seem to take any interest in any kind of rational amusement. So the other boys used to try to reason it out and come to an understanding of him, but they couldn't arrive at any satisfactory conclusion; as I said before, they could only figure out a sort of vague idea that he was 'afflicted,' and so they took him under their protection, and never allowed any harm to come to him.

This good little boy read all the Sunday-school books; they were his greatest delight. This was the whole secret of it. He believed in the good little boys they put in the Sunday-school books; he had every confidence in them. He longed to come across one of them alive, once; but he never did. They all died before his time, maybe. Whenever he read about a particularly good one, he turned over quickly to the end to see what became of him, because he wanted to travel thousands of miles and gaze on him; but it wasn't any use; that good little boy always died in the last chapter, and there was a picture of the funeral, with all his relations and the Sunday-school children standing around the grave in pantaloons that were too short, and bonnets that were too large, and everybody crying into handkerchiefs that had as much as a yard and a half of stuff in them. He was always headed off in this way. He never could see one of those good little boys, on account of his always dying in the last chapter.

Jacob had a noble ambition to be put in a Sunday-school book. He wanted to be put in, with pictures representing him gloriously declining to lie to his mother, and she weeping for joy about it; and pictures representing him standing on the doorstep giving a penny to a poor beggar-woman with six children, and telling her to spend it freely, but not to be extravagant, because extravagance is a sin;

and pictures of him magnanimously refusing to tell on the bad boy who always lay in wait for him around the corner, as he came from school, and welted him over the head with a lath, and then chased him home, saying 'Hi! hi!' as he proceeded. That was the ambition of young Jacob Blivens. He wished to be put in a Sunday-school book. It made him feel a little uncomfortable sometimes when he reflected that the good little boys always died. He loved to live, you know, and this was the most unpleasant feature about being a Sunday-school-book boy. He knew it was not healthy to be good. He knew it was more fatal than consumption to be so supernaturally good as the boys in the books were; he knew that none of them had ever been able to stand it long, and it pained him to think that if they put him in a book he wouldn't ever see it, or even if they did get the book out before he died, it wouldn't be popular without any picture of his funeral in the back part of it. It couldn't be much of a Sunday-school book that couldn't tell about the advice he gave to the community when he was dying. So, at last, of course he had to make up his mind to do the best he could under the circumstances – to live right, and hang on as long as he could, and have his dying speech all ready when his time came.

But somehow, nothing ever went right with this good little boy; nothing ever turned out with him the way it turned out with the good little boys in the books. They always had a good time, and the bad boys had the broken legs; but in his case there was a screw loose somewhere, and it all happened just the other way. When he found Jim Blake stealing apples, and went under the tree to read to him about the bad little boy who fell out of a neighbour's apple tree, and broke his arm, Jim fell out of the tree too, but he fell on *him*, and broke *his* arm, and Jim wasn't hurt at all. Jacob couldn't understand that. There wasn't anything in the books like it.

And once, when some bad boys pushed a blind man over in the mud, and Jacob ran to help him up and receive his blessing, the blind man did not give him any blessing at all, but whacked him over the head with his stick and said he would like to catch him shoving *him* again and then pretending to help him up. This was not in accordance with any of the books. Jacob looked them all over to see.

One thing that Jacob wanted to do was to find a lame dog that hadn't any place to stay, and was hungry and persecuted, and bring him home and pet him and have that dog's imperishable gratitude. And at last he found one, and was happy; and he brought him home and fed him, but when he was going to pet him the dog flew at him and tore all the clothes off him except those that were in front, and made a spectacle of him that was astonishing. He examined authorities, but he could not understand the matter. It was of the same breed of dogs that was in the books, but it acted very differently. Whatever this boy did, he got into trouble. The very things the boys in the books got rewarded for turned out to be about the most unprofitable things he could invest in.

Once when he was on his way to Sunday-school he saw some bad boys starting off pleasuring in a sailboat. He was filled with consternation, because he knew from his teaching that boys who went sailing on Sunday invariably got drowned. So he ran out on a raft to warn them, but a log turned with him and slid him into the river. A man got him out pretty soon, and the doctor pumped the water out of him and gave him a fresh start with his bellows, but he caught cold and lay sick abed nine weeks. But the most unaccountable thing about it was that the bad boys in the boat had a good time all day, and then reached home alive and well, in the most surprising manner. Jacob Blivens said there was nothing like these things in the books. He was perfectly dumbfounded.

When he got well he was a little discouraged, but he resolved to keep on trying, anyhow. He knew that so far his experiences wouldn't do to go in a book, but he hadn't yet reached the allotted term of life for good little boys, and he hoped to be able to make a record yet, if he could hold on till his time was fully up. If everything else failed, he had his dying speech to fall back on.

He examined his authorities, and found that it was now time for him to go to sea as a cabin boy. He called on a ship captain and made his application, and when the captain asked for his recommendations he proudly drew out a tract and pointed to the words: 'To Jacob Blivens, from his affectionate teacher.' But the captain was a coarse, vulgar man, and he said, 'Oh, that be blowed!' *That* wasn't any proof that he knew how to wash dishes or handle a slush-bucket, and he guessed he didn't want him.' This was altogether the most extraordinary thing that ever had happened to Jacob in all his life. A compliment from a teacher, on a tract, had never failed to move the tenderest of emotions of ship captains and open the way to all offices of honour and profit in their gift – it never had in any book that ever *he* had read. He could hardly believe his senses.

This boy always had a hard time of it. Nothing ever came out according to the authorities with him. At last, one day, when he was around hunting up bad little boys to admonish, he found a lot of them in the old iron foundry fixing up a little joke on fourteen or fifteen dogs, which they had tied together in long procession and were going to ornament with empty nitroglycerine cans made fast to their tails. Jacob's heart was touched. He sat down on one of those cans – for he never minded grease when duty was before him – and he took hold of the foremost dog by the collar, and turned his reproving eye upon wicked Tom Jones. But just at that moment Alderman McWelter, full of wrath, stepped in. All the bad boys ran away; but Jacob Blivens rose in conscious innocence and began one of those stately little Sunday-school-book speeches which always commence with 'Oh, Sir!' in dead opposition to the fact that no boy, good or bad, ever starts a remark with 'Oh, Sir!' But the Alderman never waited to hear the rest. He took Jacob Blivens by the ear and turned him around, and hit him a whack in the rear with the flat of his hand; and in an instant that good little boy shot out through the roof and soared away toward the sun, with the fragments of those fifteen dogs stringing after him like the tail of a kite. And there wasn't a sign of that Alderman or that old iron foundry left on the face of the earth; and as for young Jacob Blivens, he never got a chance to make his last dying speech after all his trouble fixing it up, unless he made it to the birds; because, although the bulk of him came down all right in a treetop in an adjoining county, the rest of him was apportioned around among four townships, and so they had to hold five inquests on him to find out whether he was dead or not, and how it occurred. You never saw a boy scattered so.

Thus perished the good little boy who did the best he could, but didn't come out according to the books. Every boy who ever did as he did prospered, except him. His case is truly remarkable. It will probably never be accounted for.

Journalism in Tennessee

The editor of the Memphis *Avalanche* swoops thus mildly
down upon a correspondent who posted him as a Radical:
'While he was writing the first word, the middle word,
dotting his i's, crossing his t's, and punching his period,
he knew he was concocting a sentence that was saturated
with infamy and reeking with falsehood.'   – *Exchange*

I was told by the physician that a Southern climate would
improve my health, and so I went down to Tennessee and
got a berth on the *Morning Glory and Johnson County War-
Whoop*, as associate editor. When I went on duty I found
the chief editor sitting tilted back in a three-legged chair
with his feet on a pine table. There was another pine table
in the room, and another afflicted chair, and both were
half buried under newspapers and scraps and sheets of
manuscript. There was a wooden box of sand, sprinkled
with cigar stubs and 'old soldiers', and a stove with a door
hanging by its upper hinge. The chief editor had a long-
tailed black cloth frock coat on, and white linen pants. His
boots were small and neatly blacked. He wore a ruffled
shirt, a large seal ring, a standing collar of obsolete pattern
and a chequered neckerchief with the ends hanging down.
Date of costume, about 1848. He was smoking a cigar and
trying to think of a word. And in trying to think of a word,

and in pawing his hair for it, he had rumpled his locks a good deal. He was scowling fearfully, and I judged that he was concocting a particularly knotty editorial. He told me to take the exchanges and skim through them and write up the 'Spirit of the Tennessee Press', condensing into the article all of their contents that seemed of interest.

I wrote as follows:

Spirit of the Tennessee Press

The editors of the *Semi-Weekly Earthquake* evidently labour under a misapprehension with regard to the Ballyhack railroad. It is not the object of the company to leave Buzzardville off to one side. On the contrary they consider it one of the most important points along the line, and consequently can have no desire to slight it. The gentlemen of the *Earthquake* will of course take pleasure in making the correction. John W. Blossom, Esq., the able editor of the Higginsville *Thunderbolt and Battle-Cry of Freedom*, arrived in the city yesterday. He is stopping at the Van Buren House.

We observe that our contemporary of the Mud Springs *Morning Howl* has fallen into the error of supposing that the election of Van Werter is not an established fact, but he will have discovered his mistake before this reminder reaches him, no doubt. He was doubtless misled by incomplete election returns.

It is pleasant to note that the city of Blathersville is endeavouring to contract with some New York gentlemen to pave its well nigh impassable streets with the Nicholson pavement. But it is difficult to accomplish a desire like this since Memphis got some New Yorkers to do a like service for her and then declined to pay for it.

However the *Daily Hurrah* still urges the measure with ability, and seems confident of ultimate success.

We are pained to learn that Col Bascom, chief editor of the *Dying Shriek for Liberty*, fell in the street a few evenings since and broke his leg. He has lately been suffering with debility, caused by overwork and anxiety on account of sickness in his family, and it is supposed that he fainted from the exertion of walking too much in the sun.

I passed my manuscript over to the chief editor for acceptance, alteration, or destruction. He glanced at it and his face clouded. He ran his eye down the pages, and his countenance grew portentous. It was easy to see that something was wrong.

Presently he sprang up and said: 'Thunder and lightning! Do you suppose I am going to speak of those cattle that way? Do you suppose my subscribers are going to stand such gruel as that? Give me the pen!'

I never saw a pen scrape and scratch its way so viciously, or plough through another man's verbs and adjectives so relentlessly. While he was in the midst of his work somebody shot at him through the open window and marred the symmetry of his ear.

'Ah,' said he, 'that is that scoundrel Smith, of the *Moral Volcano* – he was due yesterday.' And he snatched a navy revolver from his belt and fired. Smith dropped, shot in the thigh. The shot spoiled Smith's aim, who was just taking a second chance, and he crippled a stranger. It was me. Merely a finger shot off.

Then the chief editor went on with his erasures and interlineations. Just as he finished them a hand grenade came down the stovepipe, and the explosion shivered the stove into a thousand fragments. However, it did no further damage, except that a vagrant piece knocked a couple of my teeth out.

'That stove is utterly ruined,' said the chief editor.

I said I believed it was.

'Well, no matter – don't want it this kind of weather. I know the man that did it. I'll get him. Now *here* is the way this stuff ought to be written.'

I took the manuscript. It was scarred with erasures and interlineations till its mother wouldn't have known it, if it had had one. It now read as follows:

Spirit of the Tennessee Press

The inveterate liars of the *Semi-Weekly Earthquake* are evidently endeavouring to palm off upon a noble and chivalrous people another of their vile and brutal falsehoods with regard to that most glorious conception of the nineteenth century, the Ballyhack railroad. The idea that Buzzardville was to be left off at one side originated in their own fulsome brains – or rather in the settlings which *they* regard as brains. They had better swallow this lie, and not stop to chew it, either, if they want to save their abandoned, reptile carcasses the cowhiding they so richly deserve.

That ass, Blossom of the Higginsville *Thunderbolt and Battle-Cry of Freedom*, is down here again, bumming his board at the Van Buren.

We observe that the besotted blackguard of the Mud Springs *Morning Howl* is giving out, with his usual propensity for lying, that Van Werter is not elected. The heaven-born mission of journalism is to disseminate truth – to eradicate error – to educate, refine, and elevate the tone of public morals and manners; and make all men more gentle, more virtuous, more charitable, and in all ways better, and holier and happier – and yet this black-hearted villain, this hell-spawned miscreant, prostitutes his great office persistently to the dissemination of falsehood, calumny, vituperation, and degrading vulgarity. His paper is notoriously unfit to take into the people's homes, and ought to be banished to the gambling halls and brothels where the mass of reeking pollution which does duty as its editor, lives and moves, and has his being.

Blathersville wants a Nicholson pavement – it wants a jail and a poorhouse more. The idea of a pavement in a one-horse town with two gin-mills and a blacksmith shop in it, and that mustard-plaster of a newspaper, the *Daily Hurrah*! Better borrow of Memphis, where the article is cheap. The crawling insect, Buckner, who edits the *Hurrah*, is braying about this pavement business with his customary loud-mouthed imbecility, and imagining that he is talking sense. Such foul, mephitic scum as this verminous Buckner are a disgrace to journalism.

That degraded ruffian Bascom, of the *Dying Shriek for Liberty*, fell down and broke his leg yesterday – pity it wasn't his neck. He says it was 'debility caused by overwork and anxiety!' It was debility caused by trying to lug six gallons of forty-rod whisky around town when his hide is only gauged for four, and anxiety about where he was going to bum another six. He 'fainted from the exertion of walking too much in the sun!' And well he might say that – but if he would walk *straight* he would get just as far and not have to walk half as much. For years the pure air of this town has been rendered perilous by the deadly breath of this perambulating pestilence, this pulpy bloat, this steaming, animated tank of mendacity, gin, and profanity, this Bascom! Perish all such from out the sacred and majestic mission of journalism!

'Now that is the way to write – peppery and to the point. Mush-and-milk journalism gives me the fan-tods.'

About this time a brick came through the window with a splintering crash, and gave me a considerable jolt in the middle of the back. I moved out of range – I began to feel in the way. The chief said: 'That was the Colonel, likely, I've been expecting him for two days. He will be up, now, right away.'

He was correct. The 'Colonel' appeared in the door a moment afterward, with a dragoon revolver in his hand. He said: 'Sir, have I the honour of addressing the white-livered poltroon who edits this mangy sheet?'

'You have – be seated, Sir – be careful of the chair, one of the legs is gone. I believe I have the pleasure of addressing the blatant, black-hearted scoundrel, Colonel Blatherskite Tecumseh?'

'The same. I have a little account to settle with you. If you are at leisure, we will begin.'

'I have an article on the "Encouraging Progress of Moral and Intellectual Development in America," to finish, but there is no hurry. Begin.'

Both pistols rang out their fierce clamour at the same instant. The chief lost a lock of hair, and the Colonel's bullet ended its career in the fleshy part of my thigh. The Colonel's left shoulder was clipped a little. They fired again. Both missed their men this time, but I got my share, a shot in the arm. At the third fire both gentlemen were wounded slightly, and I had a knuckle chipped. I then said I believed I would go out and take a walk, as this was a private matter and I had a delicacy about participating in it further. But both gentlemen begged me to keep my seat and assured me that I was not in the way. I had thought differently, up to this time.

They then talked about the elections and the crops a while, and I fell to tying up my wounds. But presently they opened fire again with animation, and every shot took effect – but it is proper to remark that five out of the six fell to my share. The sixth one mortally wounded the Colonel, who remarked, with fine humour, that he would have to say good morning, now, as he had business up town. He then inquired the way to the undertaker's and left. The chief turned to me and said: 'I am expecting company to dinner and shall have to get ready. It will be a favour to me if you will read proof and attend to the customers.'

I winced a little at the idea of attending to the customers, but I was too bewildered by the fusillade that was still ringing in my ears to think of anything to say. He continued: 'Jones will be here at 3. Cowhide him. Gillespie will call earlier, perhaps – throw him out of the window. Ferguson will be along about 4 – kill him. That is all for today, I believe. If you have any odd time, you may write a blistering article on the police – give the Chief Inspector rats. The cowhides are under the table; weapons in the drawer – ammunition there in the corner – lint and bandages up there in the pigeonholes. In case of accident, go to Lancet, the surgeon, downstairs. He advertises – we take it out in trade.'

He was gone. I shuddered. At the end of the next three

hours I had been through perils so awful that all peace of mind and all cheerfulness had gone from me. Gillespie had called, and thrown *me* out of the window. Jones arrived promptly, and when I got ready to do the cowhiding, he took the job off my hands. In an encounter with a stranger, not in the bill of fare, I had lost my scalp. Another stranger, by the name of Thompson, left me a mere wreck and ruin of chaotic rags. And at last, at bay in the corner, and beset by an infuriated mob of editors, blacklegs, politicians, and desperadoes, who raved and swore and flourished their weapons about my head till the air shimmered with glancing flashes of steel, I was in the act of resigning my berth on the paper when the chief arrived, and with him a rabble of charmed and enthusiastic friends. Then ensued a scene of riot and carnage such as no human pen, or steel one either, could describe. People were shot, probed, dis-membered, blown up, thrown out of the window. There was a brief tornado of murky blasphemy, with a confused and frantic war dance glimmering through it, and then all was over. In five minutes there was silence, and the gory chief and I sat alone and surveyed the sanguinary ruin that strewed the floor around us. He said: 'You'll like this place when you get used to it.'

I said: 'I'll have to get you to excuse me. I think maybe I might write to suit you, after a while, as soon as I had had some practice and learned the language – I am confident I could. But to speak the plain truth, that sort of energy of expression has its inconveniences, and a man is liable to interruption. You see that, yourself. Vigorous writing is calculated to elevate the public, no doubt, but then I do not like to attract so much attention as it calls forth. I can't write with comfort when I am interrupted so much as I have been today. I like this berth well enough, but I don't like to be left here to wait on the customers. The experiences are novel, I grant you, and entertaining, too, after a fashion, but they are not judiciously distributed. A gentleman shoots at you, through the window, and cripples *me*; a bombshell comes down the stovepipe for your gratification, and sends the stove door down *my* throat; a friend drops in to swap compliments with you, and freckles *me* with bullet holes till my skin won't hold my principles; you go to dinner, and Jones comes with his cowhide, Gillespie throws me out of the window, Thompson tears all my clothes off, and an entire stranger takes my scalp with the easy freedom of an old acquaintance; and in less than five minutes all the black-guards in the country arrive in their war paint and proceed to scare the rest of me to death with their tomahawks. Take it altogether, I never have had such a spirited time in all my life as I have had today. No. I like you, and I like your calm, unruffled way of explaining things to the customers, but you see I am not used to it. The Southern heart is too impulsive – Southern hospitality is too lavish with the stranger. The paragraphs which I have written today, and into whose cold sentences your masterly hand has infused the fervent spirit of Tennesseean journalism, will wake up another nest of hornets. All that mob of editors will come – and they will come hungry, too, and want somebody for breakfast. I shall have to bid you adieu. I decline to be present at these festivities. I came South for my health – I will go back on the same errand, and suddenly. Tennessee journalism is too stirring for me.' After which, we parted, with mutual regret, and I took apartments at the hospital.

How I Edited an
Agricultural Paper Once

I did not take the temporary editorship of an agricultural paper without misgivings. Neither would a landsman take command of a ship without misgivings. But I was in circumstances that made the salary an object. The regular editor of the paper was going off for a holiday, and I accepted the terms he offered, and took his place.

The sensation of being at work again was luxurious, and I wrought all the week with unflagging pleasure. We went to press, and I waited a day with some solicitude to see whether my effort was going to attract any notice. As I left the office, toward sundown, a group of men and boys at the foot of the stairs dispersed with one impulse, and gave me passageway, and I heard one or two of them say: 'That's him!' I was naturally pleased by this incident. The next morning I found a similar group at the foot of the stairs, and scattering couples and individuals standing here and there in the street, and over the way, watching me with interest. The group separated and fell back as I approached, and I heard a man say: 'Look at his eye!' I pretended not to observe the notice I was attracting, but secretly I was pleased with it, and was purposing to write an account of it to my aunt. I went up the short flight of stairs, and heard cheery voices and a ringing laugh as I drew near the door, which I opened, and caught a glimpse of two young, rural-looking men, whose faces blanched and lengthened when they saw me, and then they both plunged through the window, with a great crash. I was surprised.

In about half an hour an old gentleman, with a flowing beard and a fine but rather austere face, entered, and sat down at my invitation. He seemed to have something on his mind. He took off his hat and set it on the floor, and got out of it a red silk handkerchief and a copy of our paper. He put the paper on his lap, and, while he polished his spectacles with his handkerchief, he said: 'Are you the new editor?'

I said I was.

'Have you ever edited an agricultural paper before?'

'No,' I said 'this is my first attempt.'

'Very likely. Have you had any experience in agriculture, practically?'

'No, I believe I have not.'

'Some instinct told me so,' said the old gentleman, putting on his spectacles and looking over them at me with asperity, while he folded his paper into a convenient shape. 'I wish to read you what must have made me have that instinct. It was this editorial. Listen, and see if it was you that wrote it: "Turnips should never be pulled – it injures them. It is much better to send a boy up and let him shake the tree."

'Now, what do you think of that? – for I really suppose you wrote it?'

'Think of it? Why, I think it is good. I think it is sense. I have no doubt that, every year, millions and millions of bushels of turnips are spoiled in this township alone by being pulled in a half-ripe condition, when, if they had sent a boy up to shake the tree—'

'Shake your grandmother! Turnips don't grow on trees!'

'Oh, they don't, don't they? Well, who said they did? The language was intended to be figurative, wholly figurative. Anybody, that knows anything, will know that I meant that the boy should shake the vine.'

Then this old person got up and tore his paper all into small shreds, and stamped on them, and broke several things with his cane, and said I did not know as much as a cow; and then went out, and banged the door after him, and, in short, acted in such a way that I fancied he was displeased about something. But, not knowing what the trouble was, I could not be any help to him.

Pretty soon after this a long, cadaverous creature, with lanky locks hanging down to his shoulders and a week's stubble bristling from the hills and valleys of his face, darted within the door, and halted, motionless, with finger on lip, and head and body bent in listening attitude. No sound was heard. Still he listened. No sound. Then he turned the key in the door, and came elaborately tiptoeing toward me, till he was within long reaching distance of me, when he stopped, and, after scanning my face with intense interest for a while, drew a folded copy of our paper from his bosom, and said: 'There – you wrote that. Read it to me, quick! Relieve me – I suffer.'

I read as follows – and as the sentences fell from my lips I could see the relief come – I could see the drawn muscles relax, and the anxiety go out of the face, and rest and peace steal over the features like the merciful moonlight over a desolate landscape:

The guano is a fine bird, but great care is necessary in rearing it. It should not be imported earlier than June nor later than September. In the winter it should be kept in a warm place, where it can hatch out its young.

It is evident that we are to have a backward season for grain. Therefore, it will be well for the farmer to begin setting out his corn-stalks and planting his buckwheat cakes in July instead of August.

Concerning the Pumpkin – This berry is a favourite with the natives of the interior of New England, who prefer it to the gooseberry for the making of fruit cake, and who likewise give it the preference over the raspberry for feeding cows, as being more filling and fully as satisfying. The pumpkin is the only esculent of the orange family that will thrive in the North, except the gourd and one or two varieties of the squash. But the custom of planting it in the front yard with the shrubbery is fast going out of vogue, for it is now generally conceded that the pumpkin, as a shade tree, is a failure.

Now, as the warm weather approaches, and the ganders begin to spawn—

The excited listener sprang toward me, to shake hands, and said: 'There, there – that will do! I know I am all right now, because you have read it just as I did, word for word. But, stranger, when I first read it this morning I said to myself, I never, never believed it before, notwithstanding my friends kept me under watch so strict, but now I believe I *am* crazy; and with that I fetched a howl that you might have heard two miles, and started out to kill somebody – because, you know, I knew it would come to that sooner or later, and so I might as well begin. I read one of them paragraphs over again, so as to be certain, and then I burned my house down and started. I have crippled several people, and have got one fellow up a tree, where I can get him if I want him. But I thought I would call in here as I passed along, and make the thing perfectly certain; and now it *is* certain, and I tell you it is lucky for the chap that is in the tree. I should have killed him, sure, as I went back. Goodbye, sir, goodbye – you have taken a great load off my mind. My reason has stood the strain of one of your agricultural articles, and I know that nothing can ever unseat it now. *Good*bye, sir.'

I felt a little uncomfortable about the cripplings and arsons this person had been entertaining himself with, for I could not help feeling remotely accessory to them; but these thoughts were quickly banished, for the regular editor walked in! [I thought to myself, Now if you had gone to Egypt, as I recommended you to, I might have had a chance to get my hand in; but you wouldn't do it, and here you are. I sort of expected you.]

The editor was looking sad, and perplexed, and dejected. He surveyed the wreck which that old rioter and these two young farmers had made, and then said: 'This is a sad business – a very sad business. There is the mucilage bottle broken, and six panes of glass, and a spittoon and two candlesticks. But that is not the worst. The reputation of the paper is injured, and permanently, I fear. True, there never was such a call for the paper before, and it never sold such a large edition or soared to such celebrity; but does one want to be famous for lunacy, and prosper upon the infirmities of his mind? My friend, as I am an honest man, the street out here is full of people, and others are roosting on the fences, waiting to get a glimpse of you, because they think you are crazy. And well they might, after reading your editorials. They are a disgrace to journalism. Why, what put it into your head that you could edit a paper of this nature? You do not seem to know the first rudiments of agriculture. You speak of a furrow and a harrow as being the same thing; you talk of the moulting season for cows; and you recommend the domestication of the polecat on account of its playfulness and its excellence as a ratter. Your remark that clams will lie quiet if music be played to them was superfluous – entirely superfluous. Nothing disturbs clams. Clams *always* lie quiet. Clams care nothing whatever about music. Ah, heavens and earth, friend, if you had made the acquiring of ignorance the study of your life, you could not have graduated with higher honour than you could today. I never saw anything like it. Your observation that the horse chestnut, as an article of commerce, is steadily gaining in favour, is simply calculated to destroy this journal. I want you to throw up your situation and go. I want no more holiday – I could not enjoy it if I had it. Certainly not with you in my chair. I would always stand in dread of what you might be going to recommend next. It makes me lose all patience every time I think of your discussing oyster-beds under the head of 'Landscape Gardening'. I want you to go. Nothing on earth could persuade me to take another holiday. Oh, why didn't you *tell* me you didn't know anything about agriculture?'

'*Tell* you, you cornstalk, you cabbage, you son of a cauliflower! It's the first time I ever heard such an unfeeling remark. I tell you I have been in the editorial business going on fourteen years, and it is the first time I ever heard of a man's having to know anything in order to edit a newspaper. You turnip! Who write the dramatic critiques for the second-rate papers? Why, a parcel of promoted shoemakers and apprentice apothecaries, who know just as much about good acting as I do about good farming and no more. Who review the books? People who never wrote one. Who do up the heavy leaders on finance? Parties who have had the largest opportunities for knowing nothing about it. Who criticise the Indian campaigns? Gentlemen who do not know a war-whoop from a wigwam, and who never have had to run a foot-race with a tomahawk or pluck arrows out of the several members of their families to build the evening campfire with. Who write the temperance appeals and clamour about the flowing bowl? Folks who will never draw another sober breath till they do it in the grave. Who edit the agricultural papers? You – yam! Men, as a general thing, who fail in the poetry line, yellow-covered novel line, sensation-drama line, city-editor line, and finally fall back on agriculture as a temporary reprieve from the poorhouse. *You* try to tell *me* anything about the newspaper business! Sir, I have been through it from Alpha to Omaha, and I tell you that the less a man knows the bigger noise he makes and the higher the salary he commands. Heaven knows if I had but been ignorant instead of cultivated, and impudent instead of diffident, I could have made a name for myself in this cold, selfish world. I take my leave, sir. Since I have been treated as you have treated me, I am perfectly willing to go. But I have done my duty. I have fulfilled my contract, as far as I was permitted to do it. I said I could make your paper of interest to all classes, and I have. I said I could run your circulation up to twenty thousand copies, and if I had had two more weeks I'd have done it. And I'd have given you the best class of readers that ever an agricultural paper had – not a farmer in it, nor a solitary individual who could tell a watermelon from a peach-vine to save his life. *You* are the loser by this rupture, not me, Pie-plant. Adios.'

I then left.

Political Economy

Political economy is the basis of all good government. The wisest men of all ages have brought to bear upon this subject the—

[Here I was interrupted and informed that a stranger wished to see me down at the door. I went and confronted him, and asked to know his business, struggling all the time to keep a tight rein on my seething political economy ideas, and not let them break away from me or get tangled in their harness. And privately I wished the stranger was in the bottom of the canal with a cargo of wheat on top of him. I was all in a fever, but he was cool. He said he was sorry to disturb me, but as he was passing he noticed that I needed some lightning-rods. I said, 'Yes, yes – go on – what about it?' He said there was nothing about it, in particular – nothing except he would like to put them up for me. I am new to housekeeping; have been used to hotels and boarding houses all my life. Like anybody else of similar experience, I try to appear (to strangers) to be an old housekeeper; consequently I said in an offhand way that I had been intending for some time to have six or eight lightning-rods put up, but— The stranger started, and looked inquiringly at me, but I was serene. I thought that if I chanced to make any mistakes he would not catch

49

me by my countenance. He said he would rather have my custom than any man's in town. I said all right, and started off to wrestle with my great subject again, when he called me back and said it would be necessary to know exactly how many 'points' I wanted put up, what parts of the house I wanted them on, and what quality of rod I preferred. It was close quarters for a man not used to the exigencies of housekeeping, but I went through creditably, and he probably never suspected that I was a novice. I told him to put up eight 'points,' and put them all on the roof, and use the best quality of rod. He said he could furnish the 'plain' article, at 20 cents a foot; 'coppered,' 25 cents; 'zinc-plated, spiral-twist,' at 30 cents, that would stop a streak of lightning anytime, no matter where it was bound, and 'render its errand harmless and its further progress apocryphal.' I said apocryphal was no slouch of a word, emanating from the source it did, but philology aside I liked the spiral-twist and would take that brand. Then he said he *could* make two hundred and fifty feet answer, but to do it right, and make the best job in town of it, and attract the admiration of the just and the unjust alike, and compel all parties to say they never saw a more symmetrical and hypothetical display of lightning-rods since they were born, he supposed he really couldn't get along without four hundred, though he was not vindictive and trusted he was willing to try. I said go ahead and use four hundred and make any kind of a job he pleased out of it, but let me get back to my work. So I got rid of him at last, and now, after half an hour spent in getting my train of political economy thoughts coupled together again, I am ready to go on once more.]

richest treasures of their genius, their experience of life, and their learning. The great lights of commercial jurisprudence, international confraternity, and biological deviation, of all ages, all civilisations, and all nationalities, from Zoroaster down to Horace Greeley, have—

[Here I was interrupted again and required to go down and confer further with that lightning-rod man. I hurried off, boiling and surging with prodigious thoughts wombed in words of such majesty that each one of them was in itself a straggling procession of syllables that might be fifteen minutes passing a given point, and once more I confronted him – he so calm and sweet, I so hot and frenzied. He was standing in the contemplative attitude of the Colossus of Rhodes, with one foot on my infant tuberose and the other among my pansies, his hands on his hips, his hat-brim tilted forward, one eye shut and the other gazing critically and admiringly in the direction of my principal chimney. He said now *there* was a state of things to make a man glad to be alive and added, 'I leave it to *you* if you ever saw anything more deliriously picturesque than eight lightning-rods on one chimney?' I said I had no present recollection of anything that transcended it. He said that in his opinion nothing on this earth but Niagara Falls was superior to it in the way of natural scenery. All that was needed now, he verily believed, to make my house a perfect balm to the eye, was to kind of touch up the other chimneys a little and thus 'add to the generous *coup d'oeil* a soothing uniformity of achievement which would allay the excitement naturally consequent upon the first *coup d'état*.' I asked him if he learned to talk out of a book, and if I could borrow it anywhere. He smiled pleasantly, and said that his manner of speaking was not taught in books, and that nothing but familiarity with lightning could enable a man to handle his conversational style with impunity. He then figured up an estimate, and said that about eight more rods scattered about my roof would about fix me right, and he guessed five hundred feet of stuff would do it and added that the first eight had got a little the start of him, so to speak, and used up a mere trifle of material more than he had calculated on – a hundred feet or along there. I said I was in a dreadful hurry, and I wished we could get this business permanently mapped out so that I could go on with my work. He said: 'I *could* have put up those eight rods, and marched off about my business – some men *would* have done it. But no, I said to myself, this man is a stranger to me and I will die before I'll wrong him; there ain't lightning-rods enough on that house, and for one I'll never stir out of my tracks till I've done as I would be done by, and told him so. Stranger, my duty is accomplished if the recalcitrant and dephlogistic messenger of heaven strikes your—' 'There, now, there,' I said, 'put on the other eight – add five hundred feet of spiral-twist – do anything and everything you want to do; but calm your sufferings and try to keep your feelings where you can reach them with the dictionary. Meanwhile, if we understand each other now, I will go to work again.' I think I have been sitting here a full hour, this time, trying to get back to where I was when my train of thought was broken up by the last inter-ruption, but I believe I have accomplished it at last and may venture to proceed again.]

wrestled with this great subject, and the greatest among them have found it a worthy adversary and one that always comes up fresh and smiling after every throw. The great Confucius said that he would rather be a profound political economist than chief of police; Cicero frequently said that political economy was the grandest consummation that the human mind was capable of consuming; and even our own Greeley has said vaguely but forcibly that—

[Here the lightning-rod man sent up another call for me. I went down in a state of mind bordering on impatience. He said he would rather have died than interrupt me, but when he was employed to do a job, and that job was expected to be done in a clean, workmanlike manner, and when it was finished and fatigue urged him to seek the rest and recreation he stood so much in need of, and he was about to do it, but looked up and saw at a glance that all the calculations had been a little out, and if a thunderstorm were to come up and that house which he felt a personal interest in stood there with nothing on earth to protect it but sixteen lightning-rods – 'Let us have peace!' I shrieked. 'Put up a hundred and fifty! Put some on the kitchen! Put a dozen on the barn! Put a couple on the cow! – put one on the cook! – scatter them all over the persecuted place till it looks like a zinc-plated, spiral-twisted, silver-mounted canebrake! Move! Use up all the material you can get your hands on, and when you run out of lightning-rods put up ram-rods, cam-rods, stair-rods, piston-rods – *anything* that will pander to your dismal appetite for artificial scenery and bring respite to my raging brain and healing to my lacerated soul!' Wholly unmoved – further than to smile sweetly – this iron being simply turned back his wristbands daintily and said he would now 'proceed to hump himself.' Well, all that was nearly three hours ago. It is questionable whether I am calm enough yet to write on the noble theme of political economy, but I cannot resist the desire to try, for it is the one subject that is nearest to my heart and dearest to my brain of all this world's philosophy.]

'Political economy is heaven's best boon to man'. When the loose but gifted Byron lay in his Venetian exile, he observed that if it could be granted him to go back and live his misspent life over again, he would give his lucid and unintoxicated intervals to the composition, not of frivolous rhymes, but of essays upon political economy. Washington loved this exquisite science; such names as Baker, Beckwith, Judson, Smith, are imperishably linked with it and even imperial Homer, in the ninth book of the Iliad, has said:

> Fiat justitia, ruat cœlum,
> Post mortem unum, ante bellum,
> Hic jacet hoc, ex-parte res,
> Politicum e-conomico est.

The grandeur of these conceptions of the old poet, together with the felicity of the wording which clothes them and the sublimity of the imagery whereby they are illustrated, have singled out that stanza and made it more celebrated than any that ever—

['Now, not a word out of you – not a single word. Just state your bill and relapse into impenetrable silence forever and ever on these premises. Nine hundred dollars? Is that all? This cheque for the amount will be honoured at any respectable bank in America. What is that multitude of people gathered in the street for? How?—"looking at the lightning-rods!" Bless my life, did they never see any lightning-rods before? Never saw "such a stack of them on one establishment," did I understand you to say? I will step down and critically observe this popular ebullition of ignorance.']

Three days later – We are all about worn out. For four-and-twenty hours our bristling premises were the talk and wonder of the town. The theatres languished, for their happiest scenic inventions were tame and commonplace compared with my lightning-rods. Our street was blocked night and day with spectators, and among them were many who came from the country to see. It was a blessed relief, on the second day, when a thunder storm came up and the lightning began to 'go for' my house, as the historian Josephus quaintly phrases it. It cleared the galleries, so to speak. In five minutes there was not a spectator within half a mile of my place; but all the high houses about that distance away were full, windows, roof, and all. And well they might be, for all the falling stars and Fourth of July fireworks of a generation put together and rained down simultaneously out of heaven in one brilliant shower upon one helpless roof, would not have any advantage of the pyro-technic display that was making my house so magnificently conspicuous in the general gloom of the storm. By actual count the lightning struck at my establishment seven hundred and sixty-four times in forty minutes, but tripped on one of those faithful rods every time and slid down the spiral-twist and shot into the earth before it probably had time to be surprised at the way the thing was done. And through all that bombardment only one patch of slates was ripped up, and that was because for a single instant the rods in the vicinity were transporting all the lightning they could possibly accommodate. Well, nothing was ever seen like it since the world began. For one whole day and night not a member of my family stuck his head out of the window but he got the hair snatched off it as smooth as a billiard-ball, and if the reader will believe me not one of us ever dreamt of stirring abroad. But at last the awful siege came to an end – because there was absolutely no more electricity left in the clouds above us within grappling distance of my insatiable rods. *Then* I sallied forth, and gathered daring workmen together, and not a bite or a nap did we take till the premises were utterly stripped of all their terrific armament except just three rods on the house, one on the kitchen, and one on the barn – and behold these remain there even unto this day. And then, and not till then, the people ventured to use our street again. I will remark here, in passing, that during that fearful time I did not continue my essay upon political economy. I am not even yet settled enough in nerve and brain to resume it.

To whom it may concern – Parties having need of three thousand two hundred and eleven feet of best quality zinc-plated spiral-twist lightning-rod stuff, and sixteen hundred and thirty-one silver-tipped points, all in tolerable repair (and, although much worn by use, still equal to any ordinary emergency), can hear of a bargain by addressing the publishers of this magazine.

The Facts Concerning the Recent Carnival of Crime in Connecticut

I was feeling blithe, almost jocund. I put a match to my cigar, and just then the morning's mail was handed in. The first superscription I glanced at was in a handwriting that sent a thrill of pleasure through and through me. It was aunt Mary's; and she was the person I loved and honoured most in all the world, outside of my own household. She had been my boyhood's idol; maturity, which is fatal to so many enchantments, had not been able to dislodge her from her pedestal; no, it had only justified her right to be there, and placed her dethronement permanently among the impossibilities. To show how strong her influence over me was, I will observe that long after everybody else's '*do-stop-smoking*' had ceased to affect me in the slightest degree, aunt Mary could still stir my torpid conscience into faint signs of life when she touched upon the matter. But all things have their limit, in this world. A happy day came at last, when even aunt Mary's words could no longer move me. I was not merely glad to see that day arrive; I was more than glad – I was grateful; for when its sun had set, the one alloy that was able to mar my enjoyment of my aunt's society was gone. The remainder of her stay with us that winter was in every way a delight. Of course she pleaded with me just as earnestly as ever, after that blessed day, to quit my pernicious habit, but to no purpose whatever; the moment she opened the subject I at once became calmly, peacefully, contentedly indifferent – absolutely, adamantinely indifferent. Consequently the closing weeks of that memorable visit melted away as pleasantly as a dream, they were so freighted, for me, with tranquil satisfaction. I could not have enjoyed my pet vice more if my gentle tormentor had been a smoker herself, and an advocate of the practice. Well, the sight of her handwriting reminded me that I was getting very hungry to see her again. I easily guessed what I should find in her letter. I opened it. Good! just as I expected; she was coming! Coming this very day, too, and by the morning train; I might expect her any moment.

I said to myself, 'I am thoroughly happy and content, now. If my most pitiless enemy could appear before me at this moment, I would freely right any wrong I may have done him.'

Straightway the door opened, and a shrivelled, shabby dwarf entered. He was not more than two feet high. He seemed to be about forty years old. Every feature and every inch of him was a trifle out of shape; and so, while one could not put his finger upon any particular part and say, 'This is a conspicuous deformity,' the spectator perceived that this little person was a deformity as a whole – a vague, general, evenly-blended, nicely-adjusted deformity. There was a fox-like cunning in the face and the sharp little eyes, and also alertness and malice. And yet, this vile bit of human rubbish seemed to bear a sort of remote and ill-defined resemblance to me! It was dully perceptible in the mean form, the countenance, and even the clothes, gestures, manner, and attitudes of the creature. He was a far-fetched, dim suggestion of a burlesque upon me, a caricature of me in little. One thing about him struck me forcibly, and most unpleasantly: he was covered all over with a fuzzy, greenish mould, such as one sometimes sees upon mildewed bread. The sight of it was nauseating.

He stepped along with a chipper air, and flung himself into a doll's chair in a very free and easy way, without waiting to be asked. He tossed his hat into the waste basket. He picked up my old chalk pipe from the floor, gave the stem a wipe or two on his knee, filled the bowl from the tobacco box at his side, and said to me in a tone of pert command, 'Gimme a match!'

I blushed to the roots of my hair; partly with indignation, but mainly because it somehow seemed to me that this whole performance was very like an exaggeration of conduct which I myself had sometimes been guilty of in my intercourse with familiar friends – but never, never with strangers, I observed to myself. I wanted to kick the pygmy into the fire, but some incomprehensible sense of being legally and legitimately under his authority forced me to obey his order. He applied the match to the pipe, took a contemplative whiff or two, and remarked, in an irritatingly familiar way, 'Seems to me it's devilish odd weather for this time of year.'

I flushed again, and in anger and humiliation as before; for the language was hardly an exaggeration of some that I have uttered in my day, and moreover was delivered in a tone of voice and with an exasperating drawl that had the seeming of a deliberate travesty of my style. Now there is nothing I am quite so sensitive about as a mocking imitation of my drawling infirmity of speech. I spoke up sharply and said, 'Look here, you miserable ash-cat! you will have to give a little more attention to your manners, or I will throw you out of the window!'

The manikin smiled a smile of malicious content and security, puffed a whiff of smoke contemptuously toward me, and said, with a still more elaborate drawl, 'Come – go gently, now; don't put on *too* many airs with your betters.'

This cool snub rasped me all over, but it seemed to subjugate me, too, for a moment. The pygmy contemplated me a while with his weasel eyes, and then said, in a peculiarly sneering way, 'You turned a tramp away from your door this morning.'

I said crustily, 'Perhaps I did, perhaps I didn't. How do *you* know?'

'Well, I know. It isn't any matter *how* I know.'

'Very well. Suppose I *did* turn a tramp away from the door – what of it?'

'Oh, nothing; nothing in particular. Only you lied to him.'

'I *didn't*! That is, I—'

'Yes, but you did; you lied to him.'

I felt a guilty pang – in truth I had felt it forty times before that tramp had travelled a block from my door – but still I resolved to make a show of feeling slandered; so I said, 'This is a baseless impertinence. I said to the tramp—'

'There – wait. You were about to lie again. I know what you said to him. You said the cook was gone downtown and there was nothing left from breakfast. Two lies. You knew the cook was behind the door, and plenty of provisions behind *her*.'

This astonishing accuracy silenced me; and it filled me with wondering speculations, too, as to how this cub could have got his information. Of course he could have culled the conversation from the tramp, but by what sort of magic had he contrived to find out about the concealed cook? Now the dwarf spoke again: 'It was rather pitiful, rather small, in you to refuse to read that poor young woman's manuscript the other day, and give her an opinion as to its literary value; and she had come so far, too, and *so* hopefully. Now *wasn't* it?'

I felt like a cur! And I had felt so every time the thing had recurred to my mind, I may as well confess. I flushed hotly and said, 'Look here, have you nothing better to do than prowl around prying into other people's business? Did that girl tell you that?'

'Never mind whether she did or not. The main thing is, you did that contemptible thing. And you felt ashamed of it afterwards. Aha! you feel ashamed of it *now*!'

This with a sort of devilish glee. With fiery earnestness I responded, 'I told that girl, in the kindest, gentlest way, that I could not consent to deliver judgment upon anyone's manuscript, because an individual's verdict was worthless. It might underrate a work of high merit and lose it to the world, or it might overrate a trashy production and so open the way for its infliction upon the world. I said that the great public was the only tribunal competent to sit in judgment upon a literary effort, and therefore it must be best to lay it before that tribunal in the outset, since in the end it must stand or fall by that mighty court's decision anyway.'

'Yes, you said all that. So you did, you juggling, small-souled shuffler! And yet when the happy hopefulness faded out of that poor girl's face, when you saw her furtively slip beneath her shawl the scroll she had so patiently and honestly scribbled at – so ashamed of her darling now, so proud of it before – when you saw the gladness go out of her eyes and the tears come there, when she crept away so humbly who had come so—'

'Oh, peace! peace! peace! Blister your merciless tongue, haven't all these thoughts tortured me enough, without *your* coming here to fetch them back again?'

Remorse! remorse! It seemed to me that it would eat the very heart out of me! And yet that small fiend only sat there leering at me with joy and contempt, and placidly chuckling. Presently he began to speak again. Every sentence was an accusation, and every accusation a truth. Every clause was freighted with sarcasm and derision, every slow-dropping word burned like vitriol. The dwarf reminded me of times when I had flown at my children in anger and punished them for faults which a little inquiry would have taught me that others, and not they, had committed. He reminded me of how I had disloyally allowed old friends to be traduced in my hearing, and been too craven to utter a word in their defence. He reminded me of many dishonest things which I had done; of many which I had procured to be done by children and other irresponsible persons; of some which I had planned, thought upon, and longed to do, and been kept from the performance by fear of consequences only. With exquisite cruelty he recalled to my mind, item by item, wrongs and unkindnesses I had inflicted and humiliations I had put upon friends since dead, 'who died thinking of those injuries, maybe, and grieving over them,' he added, by way of poison to the stab.

'For instance,' said he, 'take the case of your younger

brother, when you two were boys together, many a long year ago. He always lovingly trusted in you with a fidelity that your manifold treacheries were not able to shake. He followed you about like a dog, content to suffer wrong and abuse if he might only be with you; patient under these injuries so long as it was your hand that inflicted them. The latest picture you have of him in health and strength must be such a comfort to you! You pledged your honour that if he would let you blindfold him no harm should come to him; and then, giggling and choking over the rare fun of the joke, you led him to a brook thinly glazed with ice, and pushed him in; and how you did laugh! Man, you will never forget the gentle, reproachful look he gave you as he struggled shivering out, if you live a thousand years! Oho! you see it now, you see it *now*!'

'Beast, I have seen it a million times, and shall see it a million more! and may you rot away piecemeal, and suffer till doomsday what I suffer now, for bringing it back to me again!'

The dwarf chuckled contentedly, and went on with his accusing history of my career. I dropped into a moody, vengeful state, and suffered in silence under the merciless lash. At last this remark of his gave me a sudden rouse: 'Two months ago, on a Tuesday, you woke up, away in the night, and fell to thinking, with shame, about a peculiarly mean and pitiful act of yours toward a poor ignorant Indian in the wilds of the Rocky Mountains in the winter of eighteen hundred and—'

'Stop a moment, devil! Stop! Do you mean to tell me that even my very *thoughts* are not hidden from you?'

'It seems to look like that. Didn't you think the thoughts I have just mentioned?'

'If I didn't, I wish I may never breathe again! Look here, friend – look me in the eye. Who are you?'

'Well, who do you think?'

'I think you are Satan himself. I think you are the devil.'

'No.'

'No? Then who *can* you be?'

'Would you really like to know?'

'*Indeed* I would.'

'Well, I am your *Conscience*!'

In an instant I was in a blaze of joy and exultation. I sprang at the creature, roaring, 'Curse you, I have wished a hundred million times that you were tangible, and that I could get my hands on your throat once! Oh, but I will wreak a deadly vengeance on—'

Folly! Lightning does not move more quickly than my Conscience did! He darted aloft so suddenly that in the moment my fingers clutched the empty air he was already perched on the top of the high bookcase, with his thumb at his nose in token of derision. I flung the poker at him, and missed. I fired the bootjack. In a blind rage I flew from place to place, and snatched and hurled any missile that came handy; the storm of books, inkstands, and chunks of coal gloomed the air and beat about the manikin's perch relentlessly, but all to no purpose; the nimble figure dodged every shot; and not only that, but burst into a cackle of sarcastic and triumphant laughter as I sat down exhausted. While I puffed and gasped with fatigue and excitement, my Conscience talked to this effect: 'My good slave, you are curiously witless – no, I mean characteristically so. In truth, you are always consistent, always yourself, always an ass. Otherwise it must have occurred to you that if you attempted this murder with a sad heart and a heavy conscience, I would droop under the burdening influence instantly. Fool, I should have weighed a ton, and could not have budged from the floor; but instead, you are so cheerfully anxious to kill me that your Conscience is as light as a feather; hence I am away up here out of your reach. I can almost respect a mere ordinary sort of fool; but *you* – pah!'

I would have given anything, then, to be heavy-hearted, so that I could get this person down from there and take his life, but I could no more be heavy-hearted over such a desire than I could have sorrowed over its accomplishment. So I could only look longingly up at my master, and rave at the ill luck that denied me a heavy conscience the only time that I had ever wanted such a thing in my life. By and by I got to musing over the hour's strange adventure, and of course my human curiosity began to work. I set myself to framing in my mind some questions for this fiend to answer. Just then one of my boys entered, leaving the door open behind him, and exclaimed, 'My! what *has* been going on, here! The bookcase is all one riddle of—'

I sprang up in consternation, and shouted, 'Out of this! Hurry! Jump! Fly! Shut the door! Quick, or my Conscience will get away!'

The door slammed to, and I locked it. I glanced up and was grateful, to the bottom of my heart, to see that my owner was still my prisoner. I said, 'Hang you, I might have lost you! Children are the heedlessest creatures. But look here, friend, the boy did not seem to notice you at all; how is that?'

'For a very good reason. I am invisible to all but you.'

I made mental note of that piece of information with a good deal of satisfaction. I could kill this miscreant now, if I got a chance, and no one would know it. But this very reflection made me so light-hearted that my Conscience could hardly keep his seat, but was like to float aloft toward the ceiling like a toy balloon. I said, presently, 'Come, my Conscience, let us be friendly. Let us fly a flag of truce for a while. I am suffering to ask you some questions.'

'Very well. Begin.'

'Well, then, in the first place, why were you never visible to me before?'

'Because you never asked to see me before; that is, you never asked in the right spirit and the proper form before. You were just in the right spirit this time, and when you called for your most pitiless enemy I was that person by a very large majority, though you did not suspect it.'

'Well, did that remark of mine turn you into flesh and blood?'

'No. It only made me visible to you. I am unsubstantial, just as other spirits are.'

This remark prodded me with a sharp misgiving. If he was unsubstantial, how was I going to kill him? But I dissembled, and said persuasively, 'Conscience, it isn't sociable of you to keep at such a distance. Come down and take another smoke.'

This was answered with a look that was full of derision, and with this observation added: 'Come where you can get at me and kill me? The invitation is declined with thanks.'

'All right,' said I to myself; 'so it seems a spirit *can* be killed, after all; there will be one spirit lacking in this world, presently, or I lose my guess.'

Then I said aloud, 'Friend—'

'There; wait a bit. I am not your friend, I am your enemy; I am not your equal, I am your master. Call me "my lord", if you please. You are too familiar.'

'I don't like such titles. I am willing to call you *sir*. That is as far as—'

'We will have no argument about this. Just obey; that is all. Go on with your chatter.'

'Very well, my lord – since nothing but my lord will suit you – I was going to ask you how long you will be visible to me?'

'Always!'

I broke out with strong indignation: 'This is simply an outrage. That is what I think of it. You have dogged, and dogged, and *dogged* me, all the days of my life, invisible. That was misery enough; now to have such a looking thing as you tagging after me like another shadow all the rest of my days is an intolerable prospect. You have my opinion, my lord; make the most of it.'

'My lad, there was never so pleased a conscience in this world as I was when you made me visible. It gives me an inconceivable advantage. Now, I can look you straight in the eye, and call you names, and leer at you, jeer at you, sneer at you; and you know what eloquence there is in visible gesture and expression, more especially when the effect is heightened by audible speech. I shall always address you henceforth in your o–w–n s–n–i–v–e–l–l–i–n–g d–r–a–w–l – baby!'

I let fly with the coal-hod. No result. My lord said, 'Come, come! Remember the flag of truce!'

'Ah, I forgot that. I will try to be civil; and *you* try it, too, for a novelty. The idea of a *civil* conscience! It is a good joke; an excellent joke. All the consciences I have ever heard of were nagging, badgering, fault-finding, execrable savages! Yes; and always in a sweat about some poor little insignificant trifle or other – destruction catch the lot of them, *I* say! I would trade mine for the smallpox and seven kinds of consumption, and be glad of the chance. Now tell me, why *is* it that a conscience can't haul a man over the coals once, for an offence, and then let him alone? Why *is* it that it wants to keep on pegging at him, day and night and night and day, week in and week out, forever and ever, about the same old thing? There is no sense in that, and no reason in it. I think a conscience that will act like that is meaner than the very dirt itself.'

'Well, *we* like it; that suffices.'

'Do you do it with the honest intent to improve a man?'

That question produced a sarcastic smile, and this reply: 'No, sir. Excuse me. We do it simply because it is "business". It is our trade. The *purpose* of it *is* to improve the man, but *we* are merely disinterested agents. We are appointed by authority, and haven't anything to say in the matter. We obey orders and leave the consequences where they belong. But I am willing to admit this much: we *do* crowd the orders a trifle when we get a chance, which is most of the time. We enjoy it. We are instructed to remind a man a few times of an error; and I don't mind acknowledging that we try to give pretty good measure. And when we get hold of a man of a peculiarly sensitive nature, oh, but we do haze him! I have known consciences to come all the way from China and Russia to see a person of that kind put through his paces, on a special occasion. Why, I knew a man of that sort who had accidentally crippled a mulatto baby; the news went abroad, and I wish you may never commit another sin if the consciences didn't flock from all over the earth to enjoy the fun and help his master exercise him. That man walked the floor in torture for forty-eight hours, without eating or sleeping, and then blew his brains out. The child was perfectly well again in three weeks.'

'Well, you are a precious crew, not to put it too strong. I think I begin to see, now, why you have always been a trifle inconsistent with me. In your anxiety to get all the juice you can out of a sin, you make a man repent of it in three or four different ways. For instance, you found fault with me for lying to that tramp, and I suffered over that. But it was only yesterday that I told a tramp the square truth, to wit, that, it being regarded as bad citizenship to encourage vagrancy, I would give him nothing. What did you do *then*? Why, you made me say to myself, "Ah, it would have been so much kinder and more blameless to ease him off with a little white lie, and send him away feeling that if he could not have bread, the gentle treatment was at least something to be grateful for!" Well, I suffered all day about *that*. Three days before, I had fed a tramp, and fed him freely, supposing it a virtuous act. Straight off you said, "O false citizen, to have fed a tramp!" and I suffered as usual. I gave a tramp work; you objected to it – *after* the contract was made, of course; you never speak up beforehand. Next, I *refused* a tramp work; you objected to *that*. Next, I proposed to kill a tramp; you kept me awake all night, oozing remorse at every pore. Sure I was going to be right *this* time, I sent the next tramp away with my benediction; and I wish you may live as long as I do, if you didn't make me smart all night again because I didn't kill him. Is there *any* way of satisfying that malignant invention which is called a conscience?'

'Ha, ha! this is luxury! Go on!'

'But come, now, answer me that question. Is there any way?'

'Well, none that I propose to tell *you*, my son. Ass! I don't care *what* act you may turn your hand to, I can straightway whisper a word in your ear and make you think you have committed a dreadful meanness. It is my *business* – and my joy – to make you repent of *every*thing you do. If I have fooled away any opportunities it was not intentional; I beg to assure you it was not intentional.'

'Don't worry; you haven't missed a trick that *I* know of. I never did a thing in all my life, virtuous or otherwise, that I didn't repent of within twenty-four hours. In church last Sunday I listened to a charity sermon. My first impulse was to give three hundred and fifty dollars; I repented of that and reduced it a hundred; repented of that and reduced it another hundred; repented of that and reduced it another hundred; repented of that and reduced the remaining fifty to twenty-five; repented of that and came down to fifteen; repented of that and dropped to two dollars and a half; when the plate came around at last, I repented once more and contributed ten cents. Well, when I got home, I did wish to goodness I had that ten cents back again! You never *did* let me get through a charity sermon without having something to sweat about.'

'Oh, and I never shall, I never shall. You can always depend on me.'

'I think so. Many and many's the restless night I've wanted to take you by the neck. If I could only get hold of you now!'

'Yes, no doubt. But I am not an ass; I am only the saddle of an ass. But go on, go on. You entertain me more than I like to confess.'

'I am glad of that. (You will not mind my lying a little, to keep in practice.) Look here; not to be too personal, I think you are about the shabbiest and most contemptible little shrivelled-up reptile that can be imagined. I am grateful enough that you are invisible to other people, for I should die with shame to be seen with such a mildewed monkey of a conscience as *you* are. Now if you were five or six feet high, and—'

'Oh, come! who is to blame?'

'*I* don't know.'

'Why, you are; nobody else.'

'Confound you, I wasn't consulted about your personal appearance.'

'I don't care, you had a good deal to do with it, nevertheless. When you were eight or nine years old, I was seven feet high and as pretty as a picture.'

'I wish you had died young! So you have grown the wrong way, have you?'

'Some of us grow one way and some the other. You had a large conscience once; if you've a small conscience now, I reckon there are reasons for it. However, both of us are to blame, you and I. You see, you used to be conscientious about a great many things; morbidly so, I may say. It was a great many years ago. You probably do not remember it, now. Well, I took a great interest in my work, and I so enjoyed the anguish which certain pet sins of yours afflicted you with that I kept pelting at you until I rather overdid the matter. You began to rebel. Of course I began to lose ground, then, and shrivel a little – diminish in stature, get mouldy, and grow deformed. The more I weakened, the more stubbornly you fastened on to those particular sins; till at last the places on my person that represent those vices became as callous as shark skin. Take smoking, for instance. I played that card a little too long, and I lost.

When people plead with you at this late day to quit that vice, that old callous place seems to enlarge and cover me all over like a shirt of mail. It exerts a mysterious, smothering effect; and presently I, your faithful hater, your devoted Conscience, go sound asleep! Sound? It is no name for it. I couldn't hear it thunder at such a time. You have some few other vices – perhaps eighty, or maybe ninety – that affect me in much the same way.'

'This is flattering; you must be asleep a good part of your time.'

'Yes, of late years. I should be asleep *all* the time, but for the help I get.'

'Who helps you?'

'Other consciences. Whenever a person whose con- science I am acquainted with tries to plead with you about the vices you are callous to, I get my friend to give his client a pang concerning some villainy of his own, and that shuts off his meddling and starts him off to hunt personal consolation. My field of usefulness is about trimmed down to tramps, budding authoresses, and that line of goods, now; but don't you worry – I'll harry you on *them* while they last! Just you put your trust in me.'

'I think I can. But if you had only been good enough to mention these facts some thirty years ago, I should have turned my particular attention to sin, and I think that by this time I should not only have had you pretty permanently asleep on the entire list of human vices, but reduced to the size of a homeopathic pill, at that. That is about the style of conscience *I* am pining for. If I only had you shrunk down to a homeopathic pill, and could get my hands on you, would I put you in a glass case for a keepsake? No, sir. I would give you to a yellow dog! That is where *you* ought to be – you and all your tribe. You are not fit to be in society, in my opinion. Now another question. Do you know a good many consciences in this section?'

'Plenty of them.'

'I would give anything to see some of them! Could you bring them here? And would they be visible to me?'

'Certainly not.'

'I suppose I ought to have known that, without asking. But no matter, you can describe them. Tell me about my neighbour Thompson's conscience, please.'

'Very well. I know him intimately; have known him many years. I knew him when he was eleven feet high and of a faultless figure. But he is very rusty and tough and mis-shapen, now, and hardly ever interests himself about any-thing. As to his present size – well, he sleeps in a cigar box.'

'Likely enough. There are few smaller, meaner men in this region than Hugh Thompson. Do you know Robin-son's conscience?'

'Yes. He is a shade under four and a half feet high; used to be a blonde; is a brunette, now, but still shapely and comely.'

'Well, Robinson is a good fellow. Do you know Tom Smith's conscience?'

'I have known him from childhood. He was thirteen inches high, and rather sluggish, when he was two years old – as nearly all of us are, at that age. He is thirty-seven feet high, now, and the stateliest figure in America. His legs are still racked with growing pains, but he has a good time, nevertheless. Never sleeps. He is the most active and energetic member of the New England Conscience Club; is president of it. Night and day you can find him pegging away at Smith, panting with his labour, sleeves rolled up, countenance all alive with enjoyment. He has got his victim splendidly dragooned, now. He can make poor Smith imagine that the most innocent little thing he does is an odious sin; and then he sets to work and almost tortures the soul out of him about it.'

'Smith is the noblest man in all this section, and the purest; and yet is always breaking his heart because he cannot be good! Only a conscience *could* find pleasure in heaping agony upon a spirit like that. Do you know my aunt Mary's conscience?'

'I have seen her at a distance, but am not acquainted with her. She lives in the open air altogether, because no door is large enough to admit her.'

'I can believe that. Let me see. Do you know the conscience of that publisher who once stole some sketches of mine for a "series" of his, and then left me to pay the law expenses I had to incur in order to choke him off?'

'Yes. He has a wide fame. He was exhibited, a month ago, with some other antiquities, for the benefit of a recent Member of the Cabinet's conscience that was starving in exile. Tickets and fares were high, but I travelled for nothing by pretending to be the conscience of an editor, and got in for half price by representing myself to be the conscience of a clergyman. However, the publisher's conscience, which was to have been the main feature of the entertainment, was a failure as an exhibition. He was there, but what of that? The management had provided a microscope with a magnifying power of only thirty thousand diameters, and so nobody got to see him, after all. There was great and general dissatisfaction, of course, but—'

Just here there was an eager footstep on the stair; I opened the door, and my aunt Mary burst into the room. It was a joyful meeting, and a cheery bombardment of questions and answers concerning family matters ensued. By and by my aunt said, 'But I am going to abuse you a little now. You promised me, the day I saw you last, that you would look after the needs of the poor family around the corner as faithfully as I had done it myself. Well, I found out by accident that you failed of your promise. *Was* that right?'

In simple truth, I never had thought of that family a second time! And now such a splintering pang of guilt shot through me! I glanced up at my Conscience. Plainly, my heavy heart was affecting him. His body was drooping forward; he seemed about to fall from the bookcase. My aunt continued: 'And think how you have neglected my poor *protégée* at the almshouse, you dear, hard-hearted promise-breaker!' I blushed scarlet, and my tongue was tied. As the sense of my guilty negligence waxed sharper and stronger, my Conscience began to sway heavily back and forth; and when my aunt, after a little pause, said in a grieved tone, 'Since you never once went to see her, maybe it will not distress you now to know that that poor child died, months ago, utterly friendless and forsaken!' my Conscience could no longer bear up under the weight of my sufferings, but rumbled headlong from his high perch and struck the floor with a dull, leaden thump. He lay there writhing with pain and quaking with apprehension, but straining every muscle in frantic efforts to get up. In a fever of expectancy I sprang to the door, locked it, placed my back against it, and bent a watchful gaze upon my struggling master. Already my fingers were itching to begin their murderous work.

'Oh, what *can* be the matter!' exclaimed my aunt, shrinking from me, and following with her frightened eyes the direction of mine. My breath was coming in short, quick gasps now, and my excitement was almost uncontrollable. My aunt cried out, 'Oh, do not look so! You appal me! Oh, what can the matter be? What is it you see? Why do you stare so? Why do you work your fingers like that?'

'Peace, woman!' I said, in a hoarse whisper. 'Look elsewhere; pay no attention to me; it is nothing – nothing. I am often this way. It will pass in a moment. It comes from smoking too much.'

My injured lord was up, wild-eyed with terror, and trying to hobble toward the door. I could hardly breathe, I was so wrought up. My aunt wrung her hands, and said, 'Oh, I knew how it would be; I knew it would come to this at last! Oh, I implore you to crush out that fatal habit while it may yet be time! You must not, you shall not be deaf to my supplications longer!' My struggling Conscience showed sudden signs of weariness! 'Oh, promise me you will throw off this hateful slavery of tobacco!' My Conscience began to reel drowsily, and grope with his hands – enchanting spectacle! 'I beg you, I beseech you, I implore you! Your reason is deserting you! There is madness in your eye! It flames with frenzy! Oh, hear me, hear me, and be saved! See, I plead with you on my very knees!' As she sank before me my Conscience reeled again, and then drooped languidly to the floor, blinking toward me a last supplication for mercy, with heavy eyes. 'Oh, promise, or you are lost! Promise, and be redeemed! Promise! Promise and live!' With a long-drawn sigh my conquered Conscience closed his eyes and fell fast asleep!

With an exultant shout I sprang past my aunt, and in an instant I had my lifelong foe by the throat. After so many years of waiting and longing, he was mine at last. I tore him to shreds and fragments. I rent the fragments to bits. I cast the bleeding rubbish into the fire, and drew into my nostrils the grateful incense of my burnt offering. At last, and forever, my Conscience was dead!

I was a free man! I turned upon my poor aunt, who was almost petrified with terror, and shouted, 'Out of this with your paupers, your charities, your reforms, your pestilent morals! You behold before you a man whose life-conflict is done, whose soul is at peace; a man whose heart is dead to sorrow, dead to suffering, dead to remorse; a man *without a conscience*! In my joy I spare you, though I could throttle you and never feel a pang! Fly!'

She fled. Since that day my life is all bliss. Bliss, unalloyed bliss. Nothing in all the world could persuade me to have a conscience again. I settled all my old outstanding scores, and began the world anew. I killed thirty-eight persons during the first two weeks – all of them on account of ancient grudges. I burned a dwelling that interrupted my view. I swindled a widow and some orphans out of their last cow, which is a very good one, though not thoroughbred, I believe. I have also committed scores of crimes, of various kinds, and have enjoyed my work exceedingly, whereas it would formerly have broken my heart and turned my hair gray, I have no doubt.

In conclusion I wish to state, by way of advertisement, that medical colleges desiring assorted tramps for scientific purposes, either by the gross, by cord measurement, or per ton, will do well to examine the lot in my cellar before purchasing elsewhere, as these were all selected and prepared by myself, and can be had at a low rate, because I wish to clear out my stock and get ready for the spring trade.

Punch, Brothers, Punch!

Will the reader please to cast his eye over the following verses, and see if he can discover anything harmful in them?

> Conductor, when you receive a fare,
> Punch in the presence of the passenjare!
> A blue trip slip for an eight-cent fare,
> A buff trip slip for a six-cent fare,
> A pink trip slip for a three-cent fare,
> Punch in the presence of the passenjare!
>   *Chorus*
> Punch, brothers! punch with care!
> Punch in the presence of the passenjare!

I came across these jingling rhymes in a newspaper, a little while ago, and read them a couple of times. They took instant and entire possession of me. All through breakfast they went waltzing through my brain; and when, at last, I rolled up my napkin, I could not tell whether I had eaten anything or not. I had carefully laid out my day's work the day before – a thrilling tragedy in the novel which I am writing. I went to my den to begin my deed of blood. I took up my pen, but all I could get it to say was, 'Punch in the presence of the passenjare.' I fought hard for an hour, but it was useless. My head kept humming, 'A blue trip slip for an eight-cent fare, a buff trip slip for a six-cent fare,' and so on and so on, without peace or respite. The day's work was ruined – I could see that plainly enough. I gave up and drifted downtown, and presently discovered that my feet were keeping time to that relentless jingle. When I could stand it no longer I altered my step. But it did no good; those rhymes accommodated themselves to the new step and went on harassing me just as before. I returned home, and suffered all the afternoon; suffered all through an unconscious and unrefreshing dinner; suffered, and cried, and jingled all through the evening; went to bed and rolled, tossed, and jingled right along, the same as ever; got up at midnight frantic, and tried to read but there was nothing visible upon the whirling page except 'Punch! punch in the presence of the passenjare.' By sunrise I was out of my mind, and everybody marvelled and was distressed at the idiotic burden of my ravings – 'Punch! oh, punch! punch in the presence of the passenjare!'

Two days later, on Saturday morning, I arose, a tottering wreck, and went forth to fulfil an engagement with a valued friend, the Rev Mr—, to walk to the Talcott Tower, ten miles distant. He stared at me, but asked no questions. We started. Mr— talked, talked, talked – as is his wont. I said nothing; I heard nothing. At the end of a mile, Mr— said, 'Mark, are you sick? I never saw a man look so haggard and worn and absent-minded. Say something; do!'

Drearily, without enthusiasm, I said: 'Punch, brothers, punch with care! Punch in the presence of the passenjare!'

My friend eyed me blankly, looked perplexed, then said, 'I do not think I get your drift, Mark. There does not seem to be any relevancy in what you have said, certainly nothing sad; and yet – maybe it was the way you *said* the words – I never heard anything that sounded so pathetic. What is—'

But I heard no more. I was already far away with my pitiless, heartbreaking 'blue trip slip for an eight-cent fare, buff trip slip for a six-cent fare, pink trip slip for a three-cent fare; punch in the presence of the passenjare.' I do not know what occurred during the other nine miles. However, all of a sudden Mr— laid his hand on my shoulder and shouted, 'Oh, wake up! wake up! wake up! Don't sleep all day! Here we are at the Tower, man! I have talked myself deaf and dumb and blind, and never got a response. Just look at this magnificent autumn landscape! Look at it! look at it! Feast your eyes on it! You have travelled; you have seen boasted landscapes elsewhere. Come, now, deliver an honest opinion. What do you say to this?'

I sighed wearily, and murmured, 'A buff trip slip for a six-cent fare, a pink trip slip for a three-cent fare, punch in the presence of the passenjare.'

Rev Mr— stood there, very grave, full of concern, apparently, and looked long at me then he said, 'Mark, there is something about this that I cannot understand. Those are about the same words you said before; there does not seem to be anything in them, and yet they nearly break my heart when you say them. Punch in the – how is it they go?'

I began at the beginning and repeated all the lines. My friend's face lighted with interest. He said, 'Why, what a captivating jingle it is! It is almost music. It flows along so nicely. I have nearly caught the rhymes myself. Say them over just once more, and then I'll have them, sure.'

I said them over. Then Mr— said them. He made one little mistake, which I corrected. The next time and the next he got them right. Now a great burden seemed to tumble from my shoulders. That torturing jingle departed out of my brain, and a grateful sense of rest and peace descended upon me. I was light-hearted enough to sing; and I did sing for half an hour, straight along, as we went jogging homeward. Then my freed tongue found blessed speech again, and the pent talk of many a weary hour began to gush and flow. It flowed on and on, joyously, jubilantly, until the fountain was empty and dry. As I wrung my friend's hand at parting, I said, 'Haven't we had a royal good time! But now I remember, you haven't said a word for two hours. Come, come, out with something!'

The Rev Mr— turned a lacklustre eye upon me, drew a deep sigh, and said, without animation, without apparent consciousness, 'Punch, brothers, punch with care! Punch in the presence of the passenjare!'

A pang shot through me as I said to myself, 'Poor fellow, poor fellow! *he* has got it, now.'

I did not see Mr— for two or three days after that. Then, on Tuesday evening, he staggered into my presence and sank dejectedly into a seat. He was pale, worn; he was a wreck. He lifted his faded eyes to my face and said, 'Ah, Mark, it was a ruinous investment that I made in those heartless rhymes. They have ridden me like a nightmare, day and night, hour after hour, to this very moment. Since I saw you I have suffered the torments of the lost. Saturday evening I had a sudden call, by telegraph, and took the night train for Boston. The occasion was the death of a valued old friend who had requested that I should preach his funeral sermon. I took my seat in the cars and set myself to framing the discourse. But I never got beyond the opening paragraph; for then the train started and the car-wheels began their 'clack-clack-clack-clack! clack-clack-clack-clack!' and right away those odious rhymes fitted themselves to that accompaniment. For an hour I sat there and set a syllable of those rhymes to every separate and distinct clack the car-wheels made. Why, I was as fagged out, then, as if I had been chopping wood all day. My skull was splitting with headache. It seemed to me that I must go mad if I sat there any longer so I undressed and went to bed. I stretched myself out in my berth, and – well, you know what the result was. The thing went right along, just the same. 'Clack-clack-clack, a blue trip slip, clack-clack-clack, for an eight-cent fare; clack-clack-clack, a buff trip slip, clack-clack-clack, for a six-cent fare, and so on, and so on, and so on – *punch*, in the presence of the passenjare!' Sleep? Not a single wink! I was almost a lunatic when I got to Boston. Don't ask me about the funeral. I did the best I could, but every solemn individual sentence was meshed and tangled and woven in and out with 'Punch, brothers, punch with care, punch in the presence of the passenjare.' And the most distressing thing was that my *delivery* dropped into the undulating rhythm of those pulsing rhymes, and I could actually catch absent-minded people nodding *time* to the swing of it with their stupid heads. And, Mark, you may believe it or not, but before I got through, the entire assemblage were placidly bobbing their heads in solemn unison, mourners, undertaker, and all. The moment I had finished, I fled to the anteroom in a state bordering on frenzy. Of course it would be my luck to find a sorrowing and aged maiden aunt of the deceased there, who had arrived from Springfield too late to get into the church.

She began to sob, and said, ' "Oh, oh, he is gone, he is gone, and I didn't see him before he died!"

' "Yes!" I said, "he *is* gone, he *is* gone, he *is* gone – oh, *will* this suffering never cease!"

' "*You* loved him, then! Oh, you too loved him!"

' "Loved him! Loved *who*?"

' "Why, my poor George! my poor nephew!"

' "Oh – *him*! Yes – oh, yes, yes. Certainly – certainly. Punch – punch – oh, this misery will kill me!"

' "Bless you! bless you, sir, for these sweet words! *I*, too, suffer in this dear loss. Were you present during his last moments?"

' "Yes! I – *whose* last moments?"

' "His. The dear departed's."

' "Yes! Oh, yes – yes – *yes*! I suppose so, I think so, *I* don't know! Oh, certainly – I was there – *I* was there!"

' "Oh, what a privilege! what a precious privilege! And his last words – oh, tell me, tell me his last words! What did he say?"

' "He said – he said – oh, my head, my head, my head! He said – he said – he never said *any*thing but Punch, punch, *punch* in the presence of the passenjare! Oh, leave me, madam! In the name of all that is generous, leave me to my madness, my misery, my despair! – a buff trip slip for a six-cent fare, a pink trip slip for a three-cent fare – endurance *can* no fur-ther go! – *punch* in the presence of the passenjare!" '

My friend's hopeless eyes rested upon mine a pregnant minute, and then he said impressively, 'Mark, you do not say anything. You do not offer me any hope. But, ah me, it is just as well – it is just as well. You could not do me any good. The time has long gone by when words could comfort me. Something tells me that my tongue is doomed to wag forever to the jigger of that remorseless jingle. There – there it is coming on me again: a blue trip slip for an eight-cent fare, a buff trip slip for a—'

Thus murmuring faint and fainter, my friend sank into a peaceful trance and forgot his sufferings in a blessed respite.

How did I finally save him from the asylum? I took him to a neighbouring university and made him discharge the burden of his persecuting rhymes into the eager ears of the poor, unthinking students. How is it with *them*, now? The result is too sad to tell. Why did I write this article? It was for a worthy, even a noble, purpose. It was to warn you, reader, if you should come across those merciless rhymes, to avoid them – avoid them as you would a pestilence!

The Stolen White Elephant

I

The following curious history was related to me by a chance railway acquaintance. He was a gentleman more than seventy years of age, and his thoroughly good and gentle face and earnest and sincere manner imprinted the unmistakable stamp of truth upon every statement which fell from his lips. He said:

You know in what reverence the royal white elephant of Siam is held by the people of that country. You know it is sacred to kings, only kings may possess it, and that it is indeed in a measure even superior to kings, since it receives not merely honour but worship. Very well; five years ago, when the troubles concerning the frontier line arose between Great Britain and Siam, it was presently manifest that Siam had been in the wrong. Therefore every reparation was quickly made, and the British representative stated that he was satisfied and the past should be forgotten. This greatly relieved the King of Siam, and partly as a token of gratitude, but partly also, perhaps, to wipe out any little remaining vestige of unpleasantness which England might feel toward him, he wished to send the Queen a present – the sole sure way of propitiating an enemy, according to Oriental ideas. This present ought not only to be a royal one, but transcendently royal. Wherefore, what offering could be so meet as that of a white elephant? My position in the Indian civil service was such that I was deemed peculiarly worthy of the honour of conveying the present to her Majesty. A ship was fitted out for me and my servants and the officers and attendants of the elephant, and in due time I arrived in New York harbour and placed my royal charge in admirable quarters in Jersey City. It was necessary to remain awhile in order to recruit the animal's health before resuming the voyage.

All went well during a fortnight – then my calamities began. The white elephant was stolen! I was called up at dead of night and informed of this fearful misfortune. For some moments I was beside myself with terror and anxiety; I was helpless. Then I grew calmer and collected my faculties. I soon saw my course – for indeed there was but the one course for an intelligent man to pursue. Late as it was, I flew to New York and got a policeman to conduct me to the headquarters of the detective force. Fortunately I arrived in time, though the chief of the force, the celebrated Inspector Blunt, was just on the point of leaving for his home. He was a man of middle size and compact frame, and when he was thinking deeply he had a way of knitting his brows and tapping his forehead reflectively with his finger, which impressed you at once with the conviction that you stood in the presence of a person of no common order. The very sight of him gave me confidence and made me hopeful. I stated my errand. It did not flurry him in the least; it had no more visible effect upon his iron self-possession than if I had told him somebody had stolen my dog. He motioned me to a seat, and said calmly, 'Allow me to think a moment, please.'

So saying, he sat down at his office table and leaned his head upon his hand. Several clerks were at work at the other end of the room; the scratching of their pens was all the sound I heard during the next six or seven minutes. Meantime the inspector sat there, buried in thought. Finally he raised his head, and there was that in the firm lines of his face which showed me that his brain had done its work and his plan was made. Said he – and his voice was low and impressive, 'This is no ordinary case. Every step must be warily taken; each step must be made sure before the next is ventured. And secrecy must be observed – secrecy profound and absolute. Speak to no one about the matter, not even the reporters. I will take care of *them*; I will see that they get only what it may suit my ends to let them know.' He touched a bell; a youth appeared. 'Alaric, tell the reporters to remain for the present.' The boy retired.

'Now let us proceed to business – and systematically. Nothing can be accomplished in this trade of mine without strict and minute method.'

He took a pen and some paper. 'Now – name of the elephant?'

'Hassan Ben Ali Ben Selim Abdallah Mohammed Moisé Alhammal Jamsetjejeebhoy Dhuleep Sultan Ebu Bhudpoor.'

'Very well. Given name?'

'Jumbo.'

'Very well. Place of birth?'

'The capital city of Siam.'

'Parents living?'

'No – dead.'

'Had they any other issue besides this one?'

'None. He was an only child.'

87

'Very well. These matters are sufficient under that head. Now please describe the elephant, and leave out no particular, however insignificant – that is, insignificant from *your* point of view. To men in my profession there *are* no insignificant particulars; they do not exist.'

I described – he wrote. When I was done, he said, 'Now listen. If I have made any mistakes, correct me.'

He read as follows:

'Height, 19 feet; length from apex of forehead to insertion of tail, 26 feet; length of trunk, 16 feet; length of tail, 6 feet; total length, including trunk and tail, 48 feet; length of tusks, 9 feet; ears in keeping with these dimensions; footprint resembles the mark left when one up-ends a barrel in the snow; colour of the elephant, a dull white; has a hole the size of a plate in each ear for the insertion of jewellery, and possesses the habit in a remarkable degree of squirting water upon spectators and of maltreating with his trunk not only such persons as he is acquainted with, but even entire strangers; limps slightly with his right hind leg, and has a small scar in his left armpit caused by a former boil; had on, when stolen, a castle containing seats for fifteen persons, and a gold-cloth saddle-blanket the size of an ordinary carpet.'

There were no mistakes. The inspector touched the bell, handed the description to Alaric, and said, 'Have fifty thousand copies of this printed at once and mailed to every detective office and pawnbroker's shop on the continent.' Alaric retired. 'There – so far, so good. Next, I must have a photograph of the property.'

I gave him one. He examined it critically, and said, 'It must do, since we can do no better; but he has his trunk curled up and tucked into his mouth. That is unfortunate, and is calculated to mislead, for of course he does not usually have it in that position.' He touched his bell.

'Alaric, have fifty thousand copies of this photograph made, the first thing in the morning, and mail them with the descriptive circulars.'

Alaric retired to execute his orders. The inspector said, 'It will be necessary to offer a reward, of course. Now as to the amount?'

'What sum would you suggest?'

'To *begin* with, I should say – well, twenty-five thousand dollars. It is an intricate and difficult business; there are a thousand avenues of escape and opportunities of conceal-ment. These thieves have friends and pals everywhere—'

'Bless me, do you know who they are?'

The wary face, practised in concealing the thoughts and feelings within, gave me no token, nor yet the replying words, so quietly uttered: 'Never mind about that. I may, and I may not. We generally gather a pretty shrewd inkling of who our man is by the manner of his work and the size of the game he goes after. We are not dealing with a pickpocket or a hall thief, now, make up your mind to that. This property was not 'lifted' by a novice. But, as I was saying, considering the amount of travel which will have to be done, and the diligence with which the thieves will cover up their traces as they move along, twenty-five thousand may be too small a sum to offer, yet I think it worthwhile to start with that.'

So we determined upon that figure, as a beginning. Then this man, whom nothing escaped which could by any possibility be made to serve as a clue, said: 'There are cases in detective history to show that criminals have been detected through peculiarities in their appetites. Now, what does this elephant eat, and how much?'

'Well, as to *what* he eats – he will eat *anything*. He will eat a man, he will eat a Bible – he will eat anything *between* a man and a Bible.'

'Good – very good indeed, but too general. Details are necessary, details are the only valuable things in our trade. Very well – as to men. At one meal – or, if you prefer, during one day – how many men will he eat, if fresh?'

'He would not care whether they were fresh or not; at a single meal he would eat five ordinary men.'

'Very good; five men; we will put that down. What nationalities would he prefer?'

'He is indifferent about nationalities. He prefers acquaintances, but is not prejudiced against strangers.'

'Very good. Now, as to Bibles. How many Bibles would he eat at a meal?'

'He would eat an entire edition.'

'It is hardly succinct enough. Do you mean the ordinary octavo, or the family illustrated?'

'I think he would be indifferent to illustrations; that is, I think he would not value illustrations above simple letter-press.'

'No, you do not get my idea. I refer to bulk. The ordinary octavo Bible weighs about two pounds and a half, while the great quarto with the illustrations weighs ten or twelve. How many Doré Bibles would he eat at a meal?'

'If you knew this elephant, you could not ask. He would take what they had.'

'Well, put it in dollars and cents, then. We must get at it somehow. The Doré costs a hundred dollars a copy, Russia leather, bevelled.'

'He would require about fifty thousand dollars' worth – say an edition of five hundred copies.'

'Now that is more exact. I will put that down. Very well; he likes men and Bibles; so far, so good. What else will he eat? I want particulars.'

'He will leave Bibles to eat bricks, he will leave bricks to eat bottles, he will leave bottles to eat clothing, he will leave clothing to eat cats, he will leave cats to eat oysters, he will leave oysters to eat ham, he will leave ham to eat sugar, he will leave sugar to eat pie, he will leave pie to eat potatoes, he will leave potatoes to eat bran, he will leave bran to eat hay, he will leave hay to eat oats, he will leave oats to eat rice, for he was mainly raised on it. There is nothing whatever that he will not eat but European butter, and he would eat that if he could taste it.'

'Very good. General quantity at a meal – say about—'

'Well, anywhere from a quarter to half a ton.'

'And he drinks—'

'Everything that is fluid. Milk, water, whiskey, molasses, castor oil, camphene, carbolic acid – it is no use to go into particulars; whatever fluid occurs to you set it down. He will drink anything that is fluid, except European coffee.'

'Very good. As to quantity?'

'Put it down five to fifteen barrels – his thirst varies; his other appetites do not.'

'These things are unusual. They ought to furnish quite good clues toward tracing him.'

He touched the bell. 'Alaric, summon Captain Burns.'

Burns appeared. Inspector Blunt unfolded the whole matter to him, detail by detail. Then he said in the clear, decisive tones of a man whose plans are clearly defined in his head, and who is accustomed to command, 'Captain

Burns, detail Detectives Jones, Davis, Halsey, Bates, and Hackett to shadow the elephant.'

'Yes, sir.'

'Detail Detectives Moses, Dakin, Murphy, Rogers, Tupper, Higgins, and Bartholomew to shadow the thieves.'

'Yes, sir.'

'Place a strong guard – a guard of thirty picked men, with a relief of thirty – over the place from whence the elephant was stolen, to keep strict watch there night and day, and allow none to approach – except reporters – without written authority from me.'

'Yes, sir.'

'Place detectives in plain clothes in the railway, steamship, and ferry depots, and upon all roadways leading out of Jersey City, with orders to search all suspicious persons.'

'Yes, sir.'

'Furnish all these men with photograph and accompanying description of the elephant, and instruct them to search all trains and outgoing ferry-boats and other vessels.'

'Yes, sir.'

'If the elephant should be found, let him be seized, and the information forwarded to me by telegraph.'

'Yes, sir.'

'Let me be informed at once if any clues should be found – footprints of the animal, or anything of that kind.'

'Yes, sir.'

'Get an order commanding the harbour police to patrol the frontages vigilantly.'

'Yes, sir.'

'Despatch detectives in plain clothes over all the railways, north as far as Canada, west as far as Ohio, south as far as Washington.'

'Yes, sir.'

'Place experts in all the telegraph offices to listen to all messages; and let them require that all cipher despatches be interpreted to them.'

'Yes, sir.'

'Let all these things be done with the utmost secrecy – mind, the most impenetrable secrecy.'

'Yes, sir.'

'Report to me promptly at the usual hour.'

'Yes, sir.'

'Go!'

'Yes, sir.'

He was gone.

Inspector Blunt was silent and thoughtful a moment, while the fire in his eye cooled down and faded out. Then he turned to me and said in a placid voice, 'I am not given to boasting, it is not my habit but – we shall find the elephant.'

I shook him warmly by the hand and thanked him; and I *felt* my thanks, too. The more I had seen of the man the more I liked him, and the more I admired him and marvelled over the mysterious wonders of his profession. Then we parted for the night, and I went home with a far happier heart than I had carried with me to his office.

2

Next morning it was all in the newspapers, in the minutest detail. It even had additions – consisting of Detective This, Detective That, and Detective The Other's 'Theory' as to how the robbery was done, who the robbers were, and whither they had flown with their booty. There were eleven of these theories, and they covered all the possibilities; and this single fact shows what independent thinkers detectives are. No two theories were alike, or even much resembled each other, save in one striking particular, and in that one all the eleven theories were absolutely agreed. That was, that although the rear of my building was torn out and the only door remained locked, the elephant had not been removed through the rent, but by some other (undiscovered) outlet. All agreed that the robbers had made that rent only to mislead the detectives. That never would have occurred to me or to any other layman, perhaps, but it had not deceived the detectives for a moment. Thus, what I had supposed was the only thing that had no mystery about it was in fact the very thing I had gone furthest astray in. The eleven theories all named the supposed robbers, but no two named the same robbers; the total number of suspected persons was thirty-seven. The various newspaper accounts all closed with the most important opinion of all – that of Chief Inspector Blunt. A portion of this statement read as follows:

The chief knows who the two principals are, namely, 'Brick' Duffy and 'Red' McFadden. Ten days before the robbery was achieved he was already aware that it was to be attempted, and had quietly proceeded to shadow these two noted villains; but unfortunately on the night in question their track was lost, and before it could be found again the bird was flown – that is, the elephant.

Duffy and McFadden are the boldest scoundrels in the profession; the chief has reasons for believing that they are the men who stole the stove out of the detective head-quarters on a bitter night last winter – in consequence of which the chief and every detective present were in the hands of the physicians before morning, some with frozen feet, others with frozen fingers, ears, and other members.

When I read the first half of that I was more astonished than ever at the wonderful sagacity of this strange man. He not only saw everything in the present with a clear eye, but even the future could not be hidden from him. I was soon at his office, and said I could not help wishing he had had those men arrested, and so prevented the trouble and loss; but his reply was simple and unanswerable: 'It is not our province to prevent crime, but to punish it. We cannot punish it until it is committed.'

I remarked that the secrecy with which we had begun had been marred by the newspapers; not only all our facts but all our plans and purposes had been revealed; even all the suspected persons had been named; these would doubt-less disguise themselves now, or go into hiding.

'Let them. They will find that when I am ready for them my hand will descend upon them, in their secret places, as unerringly as the hand of fate. As to the newspapers, we *must* keep in with them. Fame, reputation, constant public mention – these are the detective's bread and butter. He must publish his facts, else he will be supposed to have none; he must publish his theory, for nothing is so strange or striking as a detective's theory, or brings him so much wondering respect; we must publish our plans, for these the journals insist upon having, and we could not deny them without offending. We must constantly show the public what we are doing, or they will believe we are doing nothing. It is much pleasanter to have a newspaper say, "Inspector Blunt's ingenious and extraordinary theory is as follows," than to have it say some harsh thing, or, worse still, some sarcastic one.'

'I see the force of what you say. But I noticed that in one part of your remarks in the papers this morning you refused to reveal your opinion upon a certain minor point.'

'Yes, we always do that; it has a good effect. Besides, I had not formed any opinion on that point, anyway.'

I deposited a considerable sum of money with the inspector, to meet current expenses, and sat down to wait for news. We were expecting the telegrams to begin to arrive at any moment now. Meantime I reread the newspapers and also our descriptive circular, and observed that our $25,000 reward seemed to be offered only to detectives. I said I thought it ought to be offered to anybody who would catch the elephant. The inspector said: 'It is the detectives who will find the elephant, hence the reward will go to the right place. If other people found the animal, it would only be by watching the detectives and taking advantage of clues and indications stolen from them, and that would entitle the detectives to the reward, after all. The proper office of a reward is to stimulate the men who deliver up their time and their trained sagacities to this sort of work, and not to confer benefits upon chance citizens who stumble upon a capture without having earned the benefits by their own merits and labours.'

This was reasonable enough, certainly. Now the telegraphic machine in the corner began to click, and the following despatch was the result:

FLOWER STATION, N.Y., 7.30 A.M.
Have got a clue. Found a succession of deep tracks across a farm near here. Followed them two miles east without result; think elephant went west. Shall now shadow him in that direction.

DARLEY, *Detective*

'Darley's one of the best men on the force,' said the inspector. 'We shall hear from him again before long.'
Telegram No. 2 came:

BARKER'S, N.J., 7.40 A.M.
Just arrived. Glass factory broken open here during night, and eight hundred bottles taken. Only water in large quantity near here is five miles distant. Shall strike for there. Elephant will be thirsty. Bottles were empty.

BAKER, *Detective*

'That promises well, too,' said the inspector. 'I told you the creature's appetites would not be bad clues.'
Telegram No. 3:

TAYLORVILLE, L.I., 8.15 A.M.
A haystack near here disappeared during night. Probably eaten. Have got a clue, and am off.

HUBBARD, *Detective*

'How he does move around!' said the inspector. 'I knew we had a difficult job on hand, but we shall catch him yet.'

FLOWER STATION, N.Y., 9 A.M.
Shadowed the tracks three miles westward. Large, deep, and ragged. Have just met a farmer who says they are not elephant tracks. Says they are holes where he dug up saplings for shade-trees when ground was frozen last winter. Give me orders how to proceed.

DARLEY, *Detective*

'Aha! a confederate of the thieves! The thing grows warm,' said the inspector.

He dictated the following telegram to Darley:

Arrest the man and force him to name his pals. Continue to follow the tracks – to the Pacific, if necessary.

Chief BLUNT

Next telegram:

CONEY POINT, PA., 8.45 A.M.
Gas office broken open here during night and three months' unpaid gas bills taken. Have got a clue and am away. MURPHY, *Detective*

'Heavens!' said the inspector; 'would he eat gas bills?'
'Through ignorance – yes; but they cannot support life. At least, unassisted.'

Now came this exciting telegram:

IRONVILLE, N.Y. 9.30 A.M.
Just arrived. This village in consternation. Elephant passed through here at five this morning. Some say he went east, some say west, some north, some south – but all say they did not wait to notice particularly. He killed a horse; have secured a piece of it for a clue. Killed it with his trunk; from style of blow, think he struck it left-

98

handed. From position in which horse lies, think elephant travelled northward along line of Berkley railway. Has four and a half hours' start, but I move on his track at once.   HAWES, *Detective*

I uttered exclamations of joy. The inspector was as self-contained as a graven image. He calmly touched his bell.

'Alaric, send Captain Burns here.'

Burns appeared.

'How many men are ready for instant orders?'

'Ninety-six, sir.'

'Send them north at once. Let them concentrate along the line of the Berkley road north of Ironville.'

'Yes, sir.'

'Let them conduct their movements with the utmost secrecy. As fast as others are at liberty, hold them for orders.'

'Yes, sir.'

'Go!'

'Yes, sir.'

Presently came another telegram:

SAGE CORNERS, N.Y., 10.30 A.M.
Just arrived. Elephant passed through here at 8. 15. All escaped from the town but a policeman. Apparently elephant did not strike at policeman, but at the lamp-post. Got both. I have secured a portion of the policeman as clue.   STUMM, *Detective*

'So the elephant has turned westward,' said the inspector. 'However, he will not escape, for my men are scattered all over that region.'

The next telegram said:

Glover's, 11.15 a.m.

Just arrived. Village deserted, except sick and aged. Elephant passed through three quarters of an hour ago. The anti-temperance mass meeting was in session; he put his trunk in at a window and washed it out with water from cistern. Some swallowed it – since dead; several drowned. Detectives Cross and O'Shaughnessy were passing through town, but going south – so missed elephant. Whole region for many miles around in terror – people flying from their homes. Wherever they turn they meet elephant, and many are killed.

Brant, *Detective*

I could have shed tears, this havoc so distressed me. But the inspector only said, 'You see – we are closing in on him. He feels our presence; he has turned eastward again.'

Yet further troublous news was in store for us. The telegraph brought this:

Hoganport, 12.19 p.m.

Just arrived. Elephant passed through half an hour ago, creating wildest fright and excitement. Elephant raged around streets; two plumbers going by, killed one – other escaped. Regret general.

O'Flaherty, *Detective*

'Now he is right in the midst of my men,' said the inspector. 'Nothing can save him.'

A succession of telegrams came from detectives who were scattered through New Jersey and Pennsylvania, and who were following clues consisting of ravaged barns, factories, and Sunday-school libraries, with high hopes – hopes amounting to certainties, indeed. The inspector said, 'I wish I could communicate with them and order them north, but that is impossible. A detective only visits a telegraph office to send his report; then he is off again, and you don't know where to put your hand on him.'

Now came this despatch:

BRIDGEPORT, CT., 12.15 P.M.
Barnum offers rate of $4,000 a year for exclusive privilege of using elephant as travelling advertising medium from now till detectives find him. Wants to paste circus-posters on him. Desires immediate answer.

BOGGS, *Detective*

'That is perfectly absurd!' I exclaimed. 'Of course it is,' said the inspector. 'Evidently Mr Barnum, who thinks he is so sharp, does not know me – but I know him.'

Then he dictated this answer to the despatch:

Mr Barnum's offer declined. Make it $7,000 or nothing.

Chief BLUNT

'There. We shall not have to wait long for an answer. Mr Barnum is not at home; he is in the telegraph office – it is his way when he has business on hand. Inside of three—'

Done. – P. T. BARNUM.

So interrupted the clicking telegraphic instrument. Before I could make a comment upon this extraordinary episode, the following despatch carried my thoughts into another and very distressing channel:

BOLIVIA, N.Y., 12.50 P.M.
Elephant arrived here from the south and passed through toward the forest at 11.50, dispersing a funeral on the

way, and diminishing the mourners by two. Citizens fired some small cannonballs into him, and then fled. Detective Burke and I arrived ten minutes later, from the north, but mistook some excavations for footprints, and so lost a good deal of time; but at last we struck the right trail and followed it to the woods. We then got down on our hands and knees and continued to keep a sharp eye on the track, and so shadowed it into the brush. Burke was in advance. Unfortunately the animal had stopped to rest; therefore, Burke having his head down, intent upon the track, burred up against the elephant's hind legs before he was aware of his vicinity. Burke instantly rose to his feet, seized the tail, and exclaimed joyfully, 'I claim the re—' but got no further, for a single blow of the huge trunk laid the brave fellow's fragments low in death. I fled rearward, and the elephant turned and shadowed me to the edge of the wood, making tremendous speed, and I should inevitably have been lost, but that the remains of the funeral providentially intervened again and diverted his attention. I have just learned that nothing of that funeral is now left; but this is no loss, for there is an abundance of material for another. Meantime, the elephant has disappeared again. MULROONEY, *Detective*

We heard no news except from the diligent and confident detectives scattered about New Jersey, Pennsylvania, Delaware, and Virginia – who were all following fresh and encouraging clues – until shortly after 2 p.m., when this telegram came:

BAXTER CENTER, 2.15 P.M.
Elephant been here, plastered over with circus-bills, and broke up a revival, striking down and damaging many

who were on the point of entering upon a better life. Citizens penned him up, and established a guard. When Detective Brown and I arrived, sometime after, we entered enclosure and proceeded to identify elephant by photograph and description. All marks tallied exactly except one, which we could not see – the boil-scar under armpit. To make sure, Brown crept under to look, and was immediately brained – that is, head crushed and destroyed, though nothing issued from debris. All fled; so did elephant, striking right and left with much effect. Has escaped, but left bold blood-track from cannon-wounds. Rediscovery certain. He broke southward, through a dense forest.   BRENT, *Detective*

That was the last telegram. At nightfall a fog shut down which was so dense that objects but three feet away could not be discerned. This lasted all night. The ferry-boats and even the omnibuses had to stop running.

3

Next morning the papers were as full of detective theories as before; they had all our tragic facts in detail also, and a great many more which they had received from their telegraphic correspondents. Column after column was occupied, a third of its way down, with glaring headlines, which it made my heart sick to read. Their general tone was like this:

'THE WHITE ELEPHANT AT LARGE!
HE MOVES UPON HIS FATAL MARCH!
WHOLE VILLAGES DESERTED BY THEIR FRIGHT-
STRICKEN OCCUPANTS!
PALE TERROR GOES BEFORE HIM, DEATH AND
DEVASTATION FOLLOW AFTER!
AFTER THESE, THE DETECTIVES.
BARNS DESTROYED, FACTORIES GUTTED, HARVESTS
DEVOURED, PUBLIC ASSEMBLAGES DISPERSED,
ACCOMPANIED BY SCENES OF CARNAGE IMPOSSIBLE
TO DESCRIBE!
THEORIES OF THIRTY-FOUR OF THE MOST
DISTINGUISHED DETECTIVES ON THE FORCE!
THEORY OF CHIEF BLUNT!'

'There!' said Inspector Blunt, almost betrayed into excitement, 'this is magnificent! This is the greatest windfall that any detective organisation ever had. The fame of it will travel to the ends of the earth, and endure to the end of time, and my name with it.'

But there was no joy for me. I felt as if I had committed all those red crimes, and that the elephant was only my irresponsible agent. And how the list had grown! In one place he had 'interfered with an election and killed five repeaters.' He had followed this act with the destruction of two poor fellows, named O'Donohue and McFlannigan, who had 'found a refuge in the home of the oppressed of all lands only the day before, and were in the act of exercising for the first time the noble right of American citizens at the polls, when stricken down by the relentless hand of the Scourge of Siam.' In another, he had 'found a crazy sensation-preacher preparing his next season's heroic attacks on the dance, the theatre, and other things which can't strike back, and had stepped on him.' And in still another place he had 'killed a lightning-rod agent.' And so the list went on, growing redder and redder, and more and more heartbreaking. Sixty persons had been killed, and two hundred and forty wounded. All the accounts bore just testimony to the activity and devotion of the detectives, and all closed with the remark that 'three hundred thousand citizens and four detectives saw the dread creature, and two of the latter he destroyed.'

I dreaded to hear the telegraphic instrument begin to click again. By and by the messages began to pour in, but I was happily disappointed in their nature. It was soon apparent that all trace of the elephant was lost. The fog had enabled him to search out a good hiding place unobserved. Telegrams from the most absurdly distant points reported that a dim vast mass had been glimpsed there through the fog at such and such an hour, and was 'undoubtedly the elephant.' This dim vast mass had been glimpsed in New Haven, in New Jersey, in Pennsylvania, in interior New York, in Brooklyn, and even in the city of New York itself! But in all cases the dim vast mass had vanished quickly and left no trace. Every detective of the large force scattered over this huge extent of country sent his hourly report, and each and every one of them had a clue, and was shadowing something, and was hot upon the heels of it.

But the day passed without other result.

The next day the same.

The next just the same.

The newspaper reports began to grow monotonous with facts that amounted to nothing, clues which led to nothing, and theories which had nearly exhausted the elements which surprise and delight and dazzle.

By advice of the inspector I doubled the reward.

Four more dull days followed. Then came a bitter blow to the poor, hard-working detectives – the journalists declined to print their theories, and coldly said, 'Give us a rest.'

Two weeks after the elephant's disappearance I raised the reward to $75,000 by the inspector's advice. It was a great sum, but I felt that I would rather sacrifice my whole private fortune than lose my credit with my government. Now that the detectives were in adversity, the newspapers turned upon them, and began to fling the most stinging sarcasms at them. This gave the minstrels an idea, and they dressed themselves as detectives and hunted the elephant on the stage in the most extravagant way. The caricaturists made pictures of detectives scanning the country with spy-glasses, while the elephant, at their backs, stole apples out of their pockets. And they made all sorts of ridiculous pictures of the detective badge – you have seen that badge printed in gold on the back of detective novels, no doubt – it is a wide-staring eye, with the legend, '*We Never Sleep.*' When detectives called for a drink, the would-be facetious bar-keeper resurrected an obsolete form of expression and said, 'Will you have an eye-opener?' All the air was thick with sarcasms. But there was one man who moved calm, untouched, unaffected, through it all. It was that heart of oak, the Chief Inspector. His brave eye never drooped, his serene confidence never wavered. He always said, 'Let them rail on; he laughs best who laughs last.'

My admiration for the man grew into a species of worship. I was at his side always. His office had become an unpleasant place to me, and now became daily more and more so. Yet if he could endure it I meant to do so also; at least, as long as I could. So I came regularly, and stayed – the only outsider who seemed to be capable of it. Everybody wondered how I could; and often it seemed to me that I must desert, but at such times I looked into that calm and apparently unconscious face, and held my ground.

About three weeks after the elephant's disappearance, I was about to say one morning that I should *have* to strike my colours and retire, when the great detective arrested the thought by proposing one more superb and masterly move.

This was to compromise with the robbers. The fertility of this man's invention exceeded anything I have ever seen, and I have had a wide intercourse with the world's finest minds. He said he was confident he could compromise for $100,000 and recover the elephant. I said I believed I could scrape the amount together, but what would become of the poor detectives who had worked so faithfully? He said, 'In compromises they always get half.'

This removed my only objection. So the inspector wrote two notes, in this form:

DEAR MADAM – Your husband can make a large sum of money (and be entirely protected from the law) by making an immediate appointment with me.

Chief BLUNT

He sent one of these by his confidential messenger to the 'reputed wife' of Brick Duffy, and the other to the reputed wife of Red McFadden.

Within the hour these offensive answers came:

YE OWLD FOOL: brick McDuffys bin ded 2 yere.

BRIDGET MAHONEY

CHIEF Bat – Red McFadden is hung and in heving 18 month. Any Ass but a detective knose that.

MARY O'HOOLIGAN

'I had long suspected these facts,' said the inspector; 'this testimony proves the unerring accuracy of my instinct.'

The moment one resource failed him he was ready with another. He immediately wrote an advertisement for the morning papers, and I kept a copy of it:

A. – xwblv. 242 N. Tjnd – fz328wmlg. Ozpo – ; 2 m! ogw. MUM.

He said that if the thief was alive this would bring him to the usual rendezvous. He further explained that the usual rendezvous was a place where all business affairs between detectives and criminals were conducted. This meeting would take place at twelve the next night.

We could do nothing till then, and I lost no time in getting out of the office, and was grateful indeed for the privilege.

At 11 the next night I brought $100,000 in banknotes and put them into the chief's hands, and shortly afterward he took his leave, with the brave old undimmed confidence in his eye. An almost intolerable hour dragged to a close; then I heard his welcome tread, and rose gasping and tottered to meet him. How his fine eyes flamed with triumph! He said, 'We've compromised! The jokers will sing a different tune tomorrow! Follow me!'

He took a lighted candle and strode down into the vast vaulted basement where sixty detectives always slept, and where a score were now playing cards to while the time. I followed close after him. He walked swiftly down to the dim remote end of the place, and just as I succumbed to the pangs of suffocation and was swooning away he stumbled and fell over the outlying members of a mighty object, and I heard him exclaim as he went down, 'Our noble profession is vindicated. Here is your elephant!'

I was carried to the office above and restored with carbolic acid. The whole detective force swarmed in, and such another season of triumphant rejoicing ensued as I had never witnessed before. The reporters were called, baskets of champagne were opened, toasts were drunk, the hand shakings and congratulations were continuous and enthusiastic. Naturally the chief was the hero of the hour, and his happiness was so complete and had been so patiently and worthily and bravely won that it made me happy to see it, though I stood there a homeless beggar, my priceless charge dead, and my position in my country's service lost to me through what would always seem my fatally careless execution of a great trust. Many an eloquent eye testified its deep admiration for the chief, and many a detective's voice murmured, 'Look at him – just the king of the profession – only give him a clue, it's all he wants, and there ain't anything hid that he can't find.' The dividing of the $50,000 made great pleasure; when it was finished the chief made a little speech while he put his share in his pocket, in which he said, 'Enjoy it, boys, for you've earned it; and more than that you've earned for the detective profession undying fame.'

A telegram arrived, which read:

MONROE, MICH., 10 P.M.
First time I've struck a telegraph office in over three weeks. Have followed those footprints, horseback, through the woods, a thousand miles to here, and they get stronger and bigger and fresher every day. Don't worry – inside of another week I'll have the elephant. This is dead sure.

DARLEY, *Detective*

The chief ordered three cheers for 'Darley, one of the finest minds on the force', and then commanded that he be telegraphed to come home and receive his share of the reward.

So ended that marvellous episode of the stolen elephant. The newspapers were pleasant with praises once more, the next day, with one contemptible exception. This sheet said, 'Great is the detective! He may be a little slow in finding a little thing like a mislaid elephant – he may hunt him all day and sleep with his rotting carcass all night for three weeks, but he will find him at last – if he can get the man who mislaid him to show him the place!'

Poor Hassan was lost to me forever. The cannon-shots had wounded him fatally, he had crept to that unfriendly place in the fog, and there, surrounded by his enemies and in constant danger of detection, he had wasted away with hunger and suffering till death gave him peace.

The compromise cost me $100,000; my detective expenses were $42,000 more; I never applied for a place again under my government; I am a ruined man and a wanderer in the earth – but my admiration for that man, whom I believe to be the greatest detective the world has ever produced, remains undimmed to this day, and will so remain unto the end.

The McWilliamses and the Burglar Alarm

The conversation drifted smoothly and pleasantly along from weather to crops, from crops to literature, from literature to scandal, from scandal to religion; then took a random jump, and landed on the subject of burglar alarms. And now for the first time Mr McWilliams showed feeling. Whenever I perceive this sign on this man's dial, I comprehend it, and lapse into silence, and give him opportunity to unload his heart. Said he, with but ill-controlled emotion: 'I do not go one single cent on burglar alarms, Mr Twain – not a single cent – and I will tell you why. When we were finishing our house, we found we had a little cash left over, on account of the plumber not knowing it. I was for enlightening the heathens with it, for I was always unaccountably down on the heathen somehow; but Mrs McWilliams said no, let's have a burglar alarm. I agreed to this compromise. I will explain that whenever I want a thing, and Mrs McWilliams wants another thing, and we decide upon the thing that Mrs McWilliams wants – as we always do – she calls that a compromise. Very well: the man came up from New York and put in the alarm, and charged three hundred and twenty-five dollars for it, and said we could sleep without uneasiness now. So we did for a while –

say a month. Then one night we smelled smoke, and I was advised to get up and see what the matter was. I lit a candle, and started toward the stairs, and met a burglar coming out of a room with a basket of tinware, which he had mistaken for solid silver in the dark. He was smoking a pipe. I said, "My friend, we do not allow smoking in this room." He said he was a stranger, and could not be expected to know the rules of the house; said he had been in many houses just as good as this one, and it had never been objected to before. He added that as far as his experience went, such rules had never been considered to apply to burglars, anyway.

'I said: "Smoke along, then, if it is the custom, though I think that the conceding of a privilege to a burglar which is denied to a bishop is a conspicuous sign of the looseness of the times. But waiving all that, what business have you to be entering this house in this furtive and clandestine way, without ringing the burglar alarm?"

'He looked confused and ashamed, and said, with embarrassment: "I beg a thousand pardons. I did not know you had a burglar alarm, else I would have rung it. I beg you will not mention it where my parents may hear of it, for they are old and feeble, and such a seemingly wanton breach of the hallowed conventionalities of our Christian civilisation might all too rudely sunder the frail bridge which hangs darkling between the pale and evanescent present and the solemn great deeps of the eternities. May I trouble you for a match?"

'I said: "Your sentiments do you honour, but if you will allow me to say it, metaphor is not your best hold. Spare your thigh; this kind light only on the box, and seldom there, in fact, if my experience may be trusted. But to return to business; how did you get in here?"

' "Through a second-storey window."'

'It was even so. I redeemed the tinware at pawnbroker's rates, less cost of advertising, bade the burglar goodnight, closed the window after him, and retired to headquarters to report. Next morning we sent for the burglar-alarm man, and he came up and explained that the reason the alarm did not "go off" was that no part of the house but the first floor was attached to the alarm. This was simply idiotic: one might as well have no armour at all in battle as to have it only on his legs. The expert now put the whole second storey on the alarm, charged three hundred dollars for it, and went his way. By-and-by, one night, I found a burglar in the third storey, about to start down a ladder with a lot of miscellaneous property. My first impulse was to crack his head with a billiard cue; but my second was to refrain from this attention, because he was between me and the cue rack. The second impulse was plainly the soundest, so I refrained, and proceeded to compromise. I redeemed the property at former rates, after deducting ten per cent for use of ladder, it being my ladder, and next day we sent down for the expert once more, and had the third storey attached to the alarm, for three hundred dollars.

'By this time the "annunciator" had grown to formidable dimensions. It had forty-seven tags on it, marked with the names of the various rooms and chimneys, and it occupied the space of an ordinary wardrobe. The gong was the size of a wash-bowl, and was placed above the head of our bed. There was a wire from the house to the coachman's quarters in the stable, and a noble gong alongside his pillow.

'We should have been comfortable now but for one

defect. Every morning at five the cook opened the kitchen door, in the way of business, and rip went that gong! The first time this happened I thought the last day was come sure. I didn't think it *in* bed – no, but out of it – for the first effect of that frightful gong is to hurl you across the house, and slam you against the wall, and then curl you up, and squirm you like a spider on a stove lid, till somebody shuts that kitchen door. In solid fact, there is no clamour that is even remotely comparable to the dire clamour which that gong makes. Well, this catastrophe happened every morning regularly at five o'clock, and lost us three hours' sleep; for, mind you, when that thing wakes you, it doesn't merely wake you in spots; it wakes you all over, conscience and all, and you are good for eighteen hours of wide-awakedness subsequently – eighteen hours of the very most inconceivable wide-awakedness that you ever experienced in your life. A stranger died on our hands one time, and we vacated and left him in our room overnight. Did that stranger wait for the general judgement? *No*, sir; he got up at five the next morning in the most prompt and unostentatious way. I knew he would; I knew it mighty well. He collected his life-insurance, and lived happy ever after, for there was plenty of proof as to the perfect squareness of his death.

'Well, we were gradually fading away toward a better land, on account of our daily loss of sleep; so we finally had the expert up again, and he ran a wire to the outside of our door, and placed a switch there, whereby Thomas, the butler, could take off and put on the alarm; but Thomas always made one little mistake – he switched the alarm off at night when he went to bed, and switched it on again at daybreak in the morning, just in time for the cook to open the kitchen door, and enable that gong to slam us across the house, sometimes breaking a window with one or the other of us. At the end of a week we recognised that this switch business was a delusion and a snare. We also discovered that a band of burglars had been lodging in the house the whole time – not exactly to steal, for there wasn't much left now, but to hide from the police, for they were hot pressed, and they shrewdly judged that the detectives would never think of a tribe of burglars taking sanctuary in a house notoriously protected by the most imposing and elaborate burglar alarm in America.

'Sent down for the expert again, and this time he struck a most dazzling idea – he fixed the thing so that opening the kitchen door would take off the alarm. It was a noble idea, and he charged accordingly. But you already foresee the result. I switched on the alarm every night at bedtime, no longer trusting to Thomas's frail memory; and as soon as the lights were out the burglars walked in at the kitchen door, thus taking the alarm off without waiting for the cook to do it in the morning. You see how aggravatingly we were situated. For months we couldn't have any company. Not a spare bed in the house; all occupied by burglars.

'Finally, I got up a cure of my own. The expert answered the call, and ran another underground wire to the stable, and established a switch there, so that the coachman could put on and take off the alarm. That worked first-rate, and a season of peace ensued, during which we got to inviting company once more and enjoying life.

'But by and by the irrepressible alarm invented a new kink. One winter's night we were flung out of bed by the sudden music of that awful gong, and when we hobbled to the annunciator, turned up the gas, and saw the word "Nursery" exposed, Mrs McWilliams fainted dead away, and I came precious near doing the same thing myself. I seized my shotgun, and stood timing the coachman whilst that appalling buzzing went on. I knew that his gong had flung him out too, and that he would be along with his gun as soon as he could jump into his clothes. When I judged that the time was ripe, I crept to the room next the nursery, glanced through the window, and saw the dim outline of the coachman in the yard below, standing at a present-arms and waiting for a chance. Then I hopped into the nursery and fired, and in the same instant the coachman fired at the red flash of my gun. Both of us were successful: I crippled a nurse, and he shot off all my back hair. We turned up the gas, and telephoned for a surgeon. There was not a sign of a burglar, and no window had been raised. One glass was absent, but that was where the coachman's charge had come through. Here was a fine mystery – a burglar alarm "going off" at midnight of its own accord, and not a burglar in the neighbourhood!

'The expert answered the usual call, and explained that it was a "false alarm". Said it was easily fixed. So he overhauled the nursery window, charged a remunerative figure for it, and departed.

'What we suffered from false alarms for the next three years no stylographic pen can describe. During the first few months I always flew with my gun to the room indicated, and the coachman always sallied forth with his battery to support me. But there was never anything to shoot at – windows all tight and secure. We always sent down for the expert next day, and he fixed those particular windows so they would keep quiet a week or so, and always remembered to send us a bill about like this:

Wire	$2.15
Nipple	.75
Two hours' labour	1.50
Wax	.47
Tape	.34
Screws	.15
Recharging battery	.98
Three hours' labour	2.25
String	.02
Lard	.66
Pond's Extract	1.25
Springs, 4 @ .50	2.00
Railroad fares	7.25
	$19.77

'At length a perfectly natural thing came about – after we had answered three or four hundred false alarms – to wit, we stopped answering them. Yes, I simply rose up calmly, when slammed across the house by the alarm, calmly inspected the annunciator, took note of the room indicated, and then calmly disconnected that room from the alarm, and went back to bed as if nothing had happened. Moreover, I left that room off permanently, and did not send for the expert. Well, it goes without saying that in the course of time *all* the rooms were taken off, and the entire machine was out of service.

'It was at this unprotected time that the heaviest calamity of all happened. The burglars walked in one night and carried off the burglar alarm! Yes, sir, every hide and hair of it; ripped it out, tooth and toenail; springs, bells, gongs, battery, and all; they took a hundred and fifty miles of copper wire; they just cleaned her out, bag and baggage, and never left us a vestige of her to swear at – swear by, I mean.

'We had a time of it to get her back; but we accomplished it finally, for money. Then the alarm firm said that what we needed now was to have her put in right – with their new patent springs in the windows to make false alarms impossible, and their new patent clock attachment to take off and put on the alarm morning and night without human assistance. That seemed a good scheme. They promised to have the whole thing finished in ten days. They began work, and we left for the summer. They worked a couple of days; then *they* left for the summer. After which the burglars moved in, and began *their* summer vacation. When we returned in the fall, the house was as empty as a beer closet in premises where painters have been at work. We refurnished, and then sent down to hurry up the expert. He came up and finished the job, and said: "Now this clock is set to put on the alarm every night at 10, and take it off every morning at 5.45. All you've got to do is to wind her up every week, and then leave her alone – she will take care of the alarm herself."

'After that we had a most tranquil season during three months. The bill was prodigious, of course, and I had said I would not pay it until the new machinery had proved itself to be flawless. The time stipulated was three months. So I paid the bill, and the very next day the alarm went to buzzing like ten thousand bee swarms at ten o'clock in the morning. I turned the hands around twelve hours, according to instructions, and this took off the alarm; but there was another hitch at night, and I had to set her ahead twelve hours once more to get her to put the alarm on again. That sort of nonsense went on a week or two then the expert came up and put in a new clock. He came up every three months during the next three years, and put in a new clock. But it was always a failure. His clocks all had the same perverse defect: they *would* put the alarm on in the daytime, and they would *not* put it on at night; and if you forced it on yourself, they would take it off again the minute your back was turned.

'Now there is the history of that burglar alarm – everything just as it happened; nothing extenuated, and naught set down in malice. Yes, sir; and when I had slept nine years with burglars, and maintained an expensive burglar alarm the whole time, for their protection, not mine, and at my sole cost – for not a d—d cent could I ever get *them* to contribute – I just said to Mrs McWilliams that I had had enough of that kind of pie; so with her full consent I took the whole thing out and traded it off for a dog, and shot the dog. I don't know what *you* think about it, Mr Twain, but *I* think those things are made solely in the interest of the burglars. Yes, sir, a burglar alarm combines in its person all that is objectionable about a fire, a riot, and a harem, and at the same time has none of the compensating advantages, of one sort or another, that customarily belong with that combination. Goodbye; I get off here.'

So saying, Mr McWilliams gathered up his satchel and umbrella, and bowed himself out of the train.

A Day at Niagara

Niagara Falls is a most enjoyable place of resort. The hotels are excellent, and the prices not at all exorbitant. The opportunities for fishing are not surpassed in the country; in fact, they are not even equalled elsewhere. Because, in other localities, certain places in the streams are much better than others; but at Niagara one place is just as good as another, for the reason that the fish do not bite anywhere, and so there is no use in your walking five miles to fish when you can depend on being just as unsuccessful nearer home. The advantages of this state of things have never heretofore been properly placed before the public.

The weather is cool in summer, and the walks and drives are all pleasant and none of them fatiguing. When you start out to 'do' the Falls you first drive down about a mile, and pay a small sum for the privilege of looking down from a precipice into the narrowest part of the Niagara River. A railway 'cut' through a hill would be as comely if it had the angry river tumbling and foaming through its bottom. You can descend a staircase here a hundred and fifty feet down, and stand at the edge of the water. After you have done it, you will wonder why you did it; but you will then be too late.

The guide will explain to you, in his blood-curdling way, how he saw the little steamer, *Maid of the Mist*, descend the fearful rapids – how first one paddle-box was out of sight behind the raging billows and then the other, and at what point it was that her smokestack toppled overboard, and where her planking began to break and part asunder – and how she did finally live through the trip, after accomplishing the incredible feat of travelling seventeen miles in six minutes, or six miles in seventeen minutes, I have really forgotten which. But it was very extraordinary, anyhow. It is worth the price of admission to hear the guide tell the story nine times in succession to different parties and never miss a word or alter a sentence or a gesture.

Then you drive over to Suspension Bridge, and divide your misery between the chances of smashing down two hundred feet into the river below, and the chances of having the railway train overhead smashing down on to you. Either possibility is discomforting taken by itself, but, mixed together, they amount in the aggregate to positive unhappiness.

On the Canada side you drive along the chasm between long ranks of photographers standing guard behind their cameras ready to make an ostentatious frontispiece of you and your decaying ambulance, and your solemn crate with a hide on it which you are expected to regard in the light of a horse, and a diminished and unimportant background of sublime Niagara; and a great many people *have* the incredible effrontery or the native depravity to aid and abet this sort of crime.

Any day, in the hands of these photographers, you may see stately pictures of papa and mamma, Johnny and Bub and Sis, or a couple of country cousins, all smiling vacantly, and all disposed in studied and uncomfortable attitudes in their carriage, and all looming up in their awe-inspiring imbecility before the snubbed and diminished presentment of that majestic presence whose ministering spirits are the rainbows, whose voice is the thunder, whose awful front is veiled in clouds, who was monarch here dead and forgotten ages before this hackful of small reptiles was deemed temporarily necessary to fill a crack in the world's unnoted myriads, and will still be monarch here ages and decades of ages after they shall have gathered themselves to their blood-relations, the other worms, and been mingled with the unremembering dust.

There is no actual harm in making Niagara a background whereon to display one's marvellous insignificance in a good strong light, but it requires a sort of superhuman self-complacency to enable one to do it.

When you have examined the stupendous Horseshoe Fall till you are satisfied you cannot improve on it, you return to America by the new Suspension Bridge, and follow up the bank to where they exhibit the Cave of the Winds.

Here I followed instructions, and divested myself of all my clothing, and put on a waterproof jacket and overalls. This costume is picturesque, but not beautiful. A guide, similarly dressed, led the way down a flight of winding stairs, which wound and wound, and still kept on winding long after the thing ceased to be a novelty, and then terminated long before it had begun to be a pleasure. We were then well down under the precipice, but still considerably above the level of the river.

We now began to creep along flimsy bridges of a single plank, our persons shielded from destruction by a crazy wooden railing, to which I clung with both hands – not because I was afraid, but because I wanted to. Presently the descent became steeper, and the bridge flimsier, and sprays from the American Fall began to rain down on us in fast increasing sheets that soon became blinding, and after that our progress was mostly in the nature of groping. Now a furious wind began to rush out from behind the waterfall, which seemed determined to sweep us from the bridge and scatter us on the rocks and among the torrents below. I remarked that I wanted to go home, but it was too late. We were almost under the monstrous wall of water thundering down from above, and speech was in vain in the midst of such a pitiless crash of sound.

In another moment the guide disappeared behind the deluge, and, bewildered by the thunder, driven helplessly by the wind, and smitten by the arrowy tempest of rain, I followed. All was darkness. Such a mad storming, roaring, and bellowing of warring wind and water never crazed my ears before; I bent my head, and seemed to receive the Atlantic on my back. The world seemed going to destruction. I could not see anything, the flood poured down so savagely. I raised my head, with open mouth, and the most of the American cataract went down my throat. If I had sprung a leak now I would have been lost. And at this moment I discovered that the bridge had ceased, and we must trust for a foothold to the slippery and precipitous rocks. I never was so scared before and survived it. But we got through at last, and emerged into the open day, where we could stand in front of the laced and frothy and seething world of descending water, and look at it. When I saw how much of it there was, and how fearfully in earnest it was, I was sorry I had gone behind it.

The noble Red Man has always been a friend and darling of mine. I love to read about him in tales and legends and romances. I love to read of his inspired sagacity, and his love of the wild free life of mountain and forest, and his general nobility of character, and his stately metaphorical manner of speech, and his chivalrous love for the dusky maiden, and the picturesque pomp of his dress and accoutrements. Especially the picturesque pomp of his dress and accoutrements. When I found the shops at Niagara Falls full of dainty Indian beadwork, and stunning moccasins, and equally stunning toy figures representing human beings who carried their weapons in holes bored through their arms and bodies, and had feet shaped like a pie, I was filled with emotion. I knew that now, at last, I was going to come face to face with the noble Red Man.

A lady clerk in a shop told me, indeed, that all her grand array of curiosities were made by the Indians, and that they were plenty about the Falls, and that they were friendly, and it would not be dangerous to speak to them. And sure enough, as I approached the bridge leading over to Luna Island, I came upon a noble Son of the Forest sitting under a tree, diligently at work on a bead reticule. He wore a slouch hat and brogans, and had a short black pipe in his mouth. Thus does the baneful contact with our effeminate civilisation dilute the picturesque pomp which is so natural to the Indian when far removed from us in his native haunts.

I addressed the relic as follows: 'Is the Wawhoo-Wang-Wang of the Whack-a-Whack happy? Does the great Speckled Thunder sigh for the warpath, or is his heart contented with dreaming of the dusky maiden, the Pride of the Forest? Does the mighty Sachem yearn to drink the blood of his enemies, or is he satisfied to make bead reticules for the papooses of the paleface? Speak sublime relic of bygone grandeur – venerable ruin, speak!'

The relic said: 'An' is it mesilf, Dennis Holligan, that ye'd be takin' for a dirty Ijin, ye drawlin', lantern-jawed, spider-legged divil! By the piper that played before Moses, I'll ate ye!'

I went away from there.

By and by, in the neighbourhood of the Terrapin Tower, I came upon a gentle daughter of the aborigines in fringed and beaded buckskin moccasins and leggins, seated on a bench with her pretty wares about her. She had just carved out a wooden chief that had a strong family resemblance to a clothespin, and was now boring a hole through his abdomen to put his bow through. I hesitated a moment, and then addressed her: 'Is the heart of the forest maiden heavy? Is the Laughing Tadpole lonely? Does she mourn over the extinguished council fires of her race, and the vanished glory of her ancestors? Or does her sad spirit wander afar toward the hunting grounds whither her brave Gobbler-of-the-Lightnings is gone? Why is my daughter silent? Has she aught against the paleface stranger?'

The maiden said: 'Faix, an' is it Biddy Malone ye dare to be callin' names? Lave this, or I'll shy your lean carcass over the cataract, ye snivelling blaggard!'

I adjourned from there also.

'Confound these Indians!' I said. 'They told me they were tame; but, if appearances go for anything, I should say they were all on the warpath.'

I made one more attempt to fraternise with them, and only one. I came upon a camp of them gathered in the shade of a great tree, making wampum and moccasins, and addressed them in the language of friendship: 'Noble Red Men, Braves, Grand Sachems, War Chiefs, Squaws, and High Muck-a-Mucks, the paleface from the land of the setting sun greets you! You, Beneficent Polecat – you, Devourer of Mountains – you, Roaring Thundergust – you, Bully Boy with a Glass Eye – the paleface from beyond the great waters greets you all! War and pestilence have thinned your ranks and destroyed your once proud nation. Poker and seven-up and a vain modern expense for soap, unknown to your glorious ancestors, have depleted your purses. Appropriating, in your simplicity, the property of others has gotten you into trouble. Misrepresenting facts, in your simple innocence, has damaged your reputation with the soulless usurper. Trading for forty-rod whisky, to enable you to get drunk and happy and tomahawk your families, has played the everlasting mischief with the picturesque pomp of your dress, and here you are, in the broad light of the nineteenth century, gotten up like a rag-tag and bobtail of the purlieus of New York. For shame! Remember your ancestors! Recall their mighty deeds! Remember Uncas! – and Red Jacket! – and Hole in the Day! – and Whoopdedoodledo! Emulate their achievements ! Unfurl yourselves under my banner, noble savages, illustrious guttersnipes—'

'Down wid him!' 'Scoop the blaggard!' 'Burn him!' 'Hang him!' 'Dhround him!'

It was the quickest operation that ever was. I simply saw a sudden flash in the air of clubs, brickbats, fists, bead-baskets, and moccasins – a single flash, and they all appeared to hit me at once, and no two of them in the same place. In the next instant the entire tribe was upon me. They tore half the clothes off me; they broke my arms and legs; they gave me a thump that dented the top of my head till it would hold coffee like a saucer; and, to crown their disgraceful proceedings and add insult to injury, they threw me over the Niagara Falls, and I got wet.

About ninety or a hundred feet from the top, the remains of my vest caught on a projecting rock, and I was almost drowned before I could get loose. I finally fell, and brought up in a world of white foam at the foot of the Fall, whose celled and bubbly masses towered up several inches above my head. Of course I got into the eddy. I sailed round and round in it forty-four times – chasing a chip and gaining on it – each round trip a half-mile – reaching for the same bush on the bank forty-four times, and just exactly missing it by a hair's-breadth every time.

At last a man walked down and sat down close to that bush and put a pipe in his mouth, and lit a match and followed me with one eye and kept the other on the match while he sheltered it in his hands from the wind. Presently a puff of wind blew it out. The next time I swept around he said: 'Got a match?'

'Yes; in my other vest. Help me out, please.'

'Not for Joe.'

When I came round again, I said: 'Excuse the seemingly impertinent curiosity of a drowning man, but will you explain this singular conduct of yours?'

'With pleasure. I am the coroner. Don't hurry on my account. I can wait for you. But I wish I had a match.'

I said: 'Take my place, and I'll go and get you one.'

He declined. This lack of confidence on his part created a coldness between us, and from that time forward I avoided him. It was my idea, in case anything happened to me, to so time the occurrence as to throw my custom into the hands of the opposition coroner on the American side.

At last a policeman came along, and arrested me for

disturbing the peace by yelling at people on shore for help. The judge fined me, but I had the advantage of him. My money was with my pantaloons, and my pantaloons were with the Indians.

Thus I escaped. I am now lying in a very critical condition. At least I am lying anyway – critical or not critical. I am hurt all over, but I cannot tell the full extent yet, because the doctor is not done taking inventory. He will make out my manifest this evening. However, thus far he thinks only sixteen of my wounds are fatal. I don't mind the others.

Upon regaining my right mind, I said: 'It is an awful savage tribe of Indians that do the beadwork and moccasins for Niagara Falls, doctor. Where are they from?'

'Limerick, my son.'

Edward Mills and George Benton: a Tale

These two were distantly related to each other – seventh cousins or something of that sort. While still babies they became orphans, and were adopted by the Brants, a childless couple, who quickly grew very fond of them. The Brants were always saying: 'Be pure, honest, sober, industrious, and considerate of others, and success in life is assured.' The children heard this repeated some thousands of times before they understood it; they could repeat it themselves long before they could say the Lord's Prayer; it was painted over the nursery door, and was about the first thing they learned to read. It was destined to become the unswerving rule of Edward Mills's life. Sometimes the Brants changed the wording a little, and said: 'Be pure, honest, sober, industrious, considerate, and you will never lack friends.'

Baby Mills was a comfort to everybody about him. When he wanted candy and could not have it, he listened to reason, and contented himself without it. When Baby Benton wanted candy he cried for it until he got it. Baby Mills took care of his toys; Baby Benton always destroyed his in a very brief time, and then made himself so insistently disagreeable that, in order to have peace in the house, little Edward was persuaded to yield up his playthings to him.

When the children were a little older, Georgie became a heavy expense in one respect: he took no care of his clothes; consequently, he shone frequently in new ones, which was not the case with Eddie. The boys grew apace. Eddie was an increasing comfort, Georgie an increasing solicitude. It was always sufficient to say, in answer to Eddie's petitions, 'I would rather you would not do it' – meaning swimming, skating, picnicking, berrying, circusing, and all sorts of things which boys delight in. But *no* answer was sufficient for Georgie; he had to be humoured in his desires, or he would carry them with a high hand. Naturally, no boy got more swimming, skating, berrying, and so forth than he; no boy ever had a better time. The good Brants did not allow the boys to play out after nine in summer evenings; they were sent to bed at that hour; Eddie honourably remained, but Georgie usually slipped out of the window toward ten, and enjoyed himself till midnight. It seemed impossible to break Georgie of this bad habit, but the Brants managed it at last by hiring him, with apples and marbles, to stay in. The good Brants gave all their time and attention to vain endeavours to regulate Georgie; they said, with grateful tears in their eyes, that Eddie needed no efforts of theirs, he was so good, so considerate, and in all ways so perfect.

By and by the boys were big enough to work, so they were apprenticed to a trade: Edward went voluntarily; George was coaxed and bribed. Edward worked hard and faithfully, and ceased to be an expense to the good Brants; they praised him, so did his master; but George ran away, and it cost Mr Brant both money and trouble to hunt him up and get him back. By and by he ran away again – more money and more trouble. He ran away a third time – and stole a few little things to carry with him. Trouble and expense for Mr Brant once more, and besides, it was with the greatest difficulty that he succeeded in persuading the master to let the youth go unprosecuted for the theft.

Edward worked steadily along, and in time became a full partner in his master's business. George did not improve; he kept the loving hearts of his aged benefactors full of trouble, and their hands full of inventive activities to protect him from ruin. Edward, as a boy, had interested himself in Sunday-schools, debating societies, penny missionary affairs, anti-tobacco organisations, anti-profanity associations, and all such things; as a man, he was a quiet but steady and reliable helper in the church, the temperance societies, and in all movements looking to the aiding and uplifting of men. This excited no remark, attracted no attention – for it was his 'natural bent'.

Finally, the old people died. The will testified their loving pride in Edward, and left their little property to George – because he 'needed it'; whereas, 'owing to a bountiful Providence', such was not the case with Edward. The property was left to George conditionally: he must buy out Edward's partner with it; else it must go to a benevolent organisation called the Prisoner's Friend Society. The old people left a letter, in which they begged their dear son Edward to take their place and watch over George, and help and shield him as they had done.

Edward dutifully acquiesced, and George became his partner in the business. He was not a valuable partner: he had been meddling with drink before; he soon developed into a constant tippler now, and his flesh and eyes showed the fact unpleasantly. Edward had been courting a sweet and kindly spirited girl for some time. They loved each other dearly, and – But about this period George began to haunt her tearfully and imploringly, and at last she went crying to Edward, and said her high and holy duty was plain before her – she must not let her own selfish desires interfere with it: she must marry 'poor George' and 'reform him'. It would break her heart, she knew it would, and so on; but duty was duty. So she married George, and Edward's heart came very near breaking, as well as her own. However, Edward recovered, and married another girl – a very excellent one she was, too.

Children came to both families. Mary did her honest best to reform her husband, but the contract was too large. George went on drinking, and by and by he fell to misusing her and the little one sadly. A great many good people strove with George – they were always at it, in fact – but he calmly took such efforts as his due and their duty and did not mend his ways. He added a vice, presently – that of secret gambling. He got deeply in debt; he borrowed money on the firm's credit, as quietly as he could, and carried this system so far and so successfully that one morning the sheriff took possession of the establishment, and the two cousins found themselves penniless.

Times were hard, now, and they grew worse. Edward moved his family into a garret, and walked the streets day and night, seeking work. He begged for it, but it was really not to be had. He was astonished to see how soon his face became unwelcome; he was astonished and hurt to see how quickly the ancient interest which people had had in him faded out and disappeared. Still, he *must* get work; so he swallowed his chagrin, and toiled on in search of it. At last he got a job of carrying bricks up a ladder in a hod, and was a grateful man in consequence; but after that *nobody* knew him or cared anything about him. He was not able to keep up his dues in the various moral organisations to which he belonged, and had to endure the sharp pain of seeing himself brought under the disgrace of suspension.

But the faster Edward died out of public knowledge and interest, the faster George rose in them. He was found lying, ragged and drunk, in the gutter one morning. A member of the Ladies' Temperance Refuge fished him out, took him in hand, got up a subscription for him, kept him sober a whole week, then got a situation for him. An account of it was published.

General attention was thus drawn to the poor fellow, and a great many people came forward, and helped him toward reform with their countenance and encouragement. He did not drink a drop for two months, and meantime was the pet of the good. Then he fell – in the gutter; and there was general sorrow and lamentation. But the noble sisterhood rescued him again. They cleaned him up, they fed him, they listened to the mournful music of his repentances, they got him his situation again. An account of this, also, was published, and the town was drowned in happy tears over the re-restoration of the poor beast and struggling victim of the fatal bowl. A grand temperance revival was got up, and after some rousing speeches had been made the chairman said, impressively: 'We are now about to call for signers, and I think there is a spectacle in store for you which not many in this house will be able to view with dry eyes.' There was an eloquent pause, and then George Benton, escorted by a red-sashed detachment of the Ladies of the Refuge, stepped forward upon the platform and signed the pledge. The air was rent with applause, and everybody cried for joy. Everybody wrung the hand of the new convert when the meeting was over; his salary was enlarged next day; he was the talk of the town, and its hero. An account of it was published.

George Benton fell regularly, every three months, but was faithfully rescued and wrought with, every time, and good situations were found for him. Finally, he was taken around the country lecturing, as a reformed drunkard, and he had great houses and did an immense amount of good.

He was so popular at home, and so trusted – during his sober intervals – that he was enabled to use the name of a principal citizen and get a large sum of money at the bank. A mighty pressure was brought to bear to save him from the consequences of his forgery and it was partially successful – he was sent up for only two years. When, at the end of a year, the tireless efforts of the benevolent were crowned with success, and he emerged from the penitentiary with a pardon in his pocket, the Prisoner's Friend Society met him at the door with a situation and a comfortable salary, and all the other benevolent people came forward and gave him advice, encouragement, and help. Edward Mills had once applied to the Prisoner's Friend Society for a situation when in dire need, but the question, 'Have you been a prisoner?' made brief work of his case.

While all these things were going on, Edward Mills had been quietly making head against adversity. He was still poor, but was in receipt of a steady and sufficient salary as the respected and trusted cashier of a bank. George Benton never came near him and was never heard to inquire about him. George got to indulging in long absences from the town; there were ill reports about him, but nothing definite.

One winter's night some masked burglars forced their way into the bank, and found Edward Mills there alone. They commanded him to reveal the 'combination,' so that they could get into the safe. He refused. They threatened his life. He said his employer trusted him and he could not be traitor to that trust. He could die if he must but while he lived he would be faithful; he would not yield up the 'combination.' The burglars killed him.

The detectives hunted down the criminals; the chief one proved to be George Benton.

A wide sympathy was felt for the widow and orphans of the dead man, and all the newspapers in the land begged that all the banks in the land would testify their appreciation of the fidelity and heroism of the murdered cashier by coming forward with a generous contribution of money in aid his family, now bereft of support. The result was a mass of solid cash amounting to upward of five hundred dollars – an average of nearly three-eighths of a cent for each bank of the Union. The cashier's own bank testified its gratitude by endeavouring to show (but humiliatingly failed in it) that the peerless servant's accounts were not square, and that he himself had knocked his brains out with a bludgeon to escape detection and punishment.

George Benton was arraigned for trial. Then everybody seemed to forget the widow and orphans in their solicitude for poor George. Everything that money and influence could do was done to save him, but it all failed; he was sentenced to death. Straightway the Governor was besieged with petitions for commutation or pardon; they were brought by tearful young girls; by sorrowful old maids; by deputations of pathetic widows; by shoals of impressive orphans. But no, the Governor – for once – would not yield.

Now George Benton experienced religion. The glad news flew all around. From that time forth his cell was always full of girls and women and fresh flowers; all the day long there was prayer, and hymn-singing, and thanksgivings, and homilies, and tears, with never an interruption, except an occasional five minute intermission for refreshments.

This sort of thing continued up the very gallows, and George Benton went proudly home, in the black cap, before a wailing audience of the sweetest and best that the region could produce. His grave had fresh flowers on it everyday, for a while, and the headstone bore these words, under a hand pointing aloft: 'He has fought the good fight.'

The brave cashier's headstone has this inscription: 'Be pure, honest, sober, industrious, considerate, and you will never—'

Nobody knows who gave the order to leave it that way, but it was so given.

The cashier's family are in stringent circumstances, now, it is said; but no matter; a lot of appreciative people, who were not willing that an act so brave and true as his should go unrewarded, have collected forty-two thousand dollars – and built a memorial Church with it.

The $30,000 Bequest

Lakeside was a pleasant little town of five or six thousand inhabitants, and a rather pretty one, too, as towns go in the Far West. It had church accommodations for 35,000, which is the way of the Far West and the South, where everybody is religious, and where each of the Protestant sects is represented and has a plant of its own. Rank was unknown in Lakeside – unconfessed, anyway; everybody knew everybody and his dog, and a sociable friendliness was the prevailing atmosphere.

Saladin Foster was bookkeeper in the principal store, and the only high-salaried man of his profession in Lakeside. He was thirty-five years old, now; he had served that store for fourteen years; he had begun in his marriage-week at four hundred dollars a year, and had climbed steadily up, a hundred dollars a year for four years; from that time forth his wage had remained eight hundred – a handsome figure indeed, and everybody conceded that he was worth it.

His wife, Electra, was a capable helpmeet, although – like himself – a dreamer of dreams and a private dabbler in romance. The first thing she did, after her marriage – child as she was, aged only nineteen – was to buy an acre of ground on the edge of the town, and pay down the cash for it – twenty-five dollars, all her fortune. Saladin had less, by fifteen. She instituted a vegetable garden there, got it farmed on shares by the nearest neighbour, and made it pay her a hundred per cent a year. Out of Saladin's first year's wage she put thirty dollars in the savings bank, sixty out of his second, a hundred out of his third, a hundred and fifty out of his fourth. His wage went to eight hundred a year, then, and meantime two children had arrived and increased the expenses, but she banked two hundred a year from the salary, nevertheless, thenceforth. When she had been married seven years she built and furnished a pretty and comfortable two-thousand-dollar house in the midst of her garden-acre, paid half of the money down, and moved her family in. Seven years later she was out of debt and had several hundred dollars out earning its living.

Earning it by the rise in landed estate; for she had long ago bought another acre or two and sold the most of it at a profit to pleasant people who were willing to build, and would be good neighbours and furnish a genial comradeship for herself and her growing family. She had an independent income from safe investments of about a hundred dollars a year; her children were growing in years and grace; and she was a pleased and happy woman. Happy in her husband, happy in her children, and the husband and the children were happy in her. It is at this point that this history begins.

The youngest girl, Clytemnestra – called Clytie for short – was eleven; her sister, Gwendolen – called Gwen for short – was thirteen; nice girls, and comely. The names betray the latent romance-tinge in the parental blood, the parents' names indicate that the tinge was an inheritance. It was an affectionate family, hence all four of its members had pet names. Saladin's was a curious and unsexing one – Sally; and so was Electra's – Aleck. All day long Sally was a good and diligent bookkeeper and salesman; all day long Aleck was a good and faithful mother and housewife, and thoughtful and calculating businesswoman; but in the cosy living room at night they put the plodding world away and lived in another and a fairer, reading romances to each other, dreaming dreams, comrading with kings and princes and stately lords and ladies in the flash and stir and splendour of noble palaces and grim and ancient castles.

2

Now came great news! Stunning news, joyous news, in fact. It came from a neighbouring state, where the family's only surviving relative lived. It was Sally's relative – a sort of vague and indefinite uncle or second or third cousin by the name of Tilbury Foster, seventy and a bachelor, reputed well-off and correspondingly sour and crusty. Sally had tried to make up to him once, by letter, in a bygone time, and had not made that mistake again. Tilbury now wrote to Sally, saying he should shortly die, and should leave him thirty thousand dollars, cash; not for love, but because money had given him most of his troubles and exasperations, and he wished to place it where there was good hope that it would continue its malignant work. The bequest would be found in his will, and would be paid over. *Provided*, that Sally should be able to prove to the executors that he had *taken no notice of the gift by spoken word or by letter, had made no inquiries concerning the moribund's progress toward the everlasting tropics, and had not attended the funeral.*

As soon as Aleck had partially recovered from the

tremendous emotions created by the letter, she sent to the relative's habitat and subscribed for the local paper.

Man and wife entered into a solemn compact, now, to never mention the great news to anyone while the relative lived, lest some ignorant person carry the fact to the deathbed and distort it and make it appear that they were disobediently thankful for the bequest, and just the same as confessing it and publishing it right in the face of the prohibition.

For the rest of the day Sally made havoc and confusion with his books, and Aleck could not keep her mind on her affairs, nor even take up a flowerpot or book or a stick of wood without forgetting what she had intended to do with it. For both were dreaming.

'Thir–ty thousand dollars!'

All day long the music of those inspiring words sang through those people's heads.

From his marriage day forth, Aleck's grip had been upon the purse, and Sally had seldom known what it was to be privileged to squander a dime on non-necessities.

'Thir-ty thousand dollars!' the song went on and on. A vast sum, an unthinkable sum!

All day long Aleck was absorbed in planning how to invest it, Sally in planning how to spend it.

There was no romance-reading that night. The children took themselves away early, for the parents were silent, distraught, and strangely unentertaining. The goodnight kisses might as well have been impressed upon vacancy, for all the response they got; the parents were not aware of the kisses, and the children had been gone an hour before their absence was noticed. Two pencils had been busy during that hour – note-making; in the way of plans. It was Sally who broke the stillness at last. He said, with exultation: 'Ah, it'll be grand, Aleck! Out of the first thousand we'll have a horse and a buggy for summer, and a cutter and a skin lap-robe for winter.'

Aleck responded, with decision and composure: 'Out of the *capital*? Nothing of the kind. Not if it was a million!'

Sally was deeply disappointed; the glow went out of his face.

'Oh, Aleck,' he said, reproachfully. 'We've always worked so hard and been so scrimped; and now that we are rich it does seem—'

He did not finish, for he saw her eye soften; his supplication had touched her. She said, with gentle persuasiveness: 'We must not spend the capital, dear, it would not be wise. Out of the income from it—'

'That will answer, that will answer, Aleck! How dear and good you are! There will be a noble income, and if we can spend that—'

'Not *all* of it, dear, not all of it, but you can spend a part of it. That is, a reasonable part. But the whole of the capital – every penny of it must be put right to work, and kept at it. You see the reasonableness of that, don't you?'

'Why, ye–s. Yes, of course. But we'll have to wait so long. Six months before the first interest falls due.'

'Yes – maybe longer.'

'Longer, Aleck! Why! Don't they pay half-yearly!'

'*That* kind of an investment – yes; but I shan't invest in that way.'

'What way then?'

'For big returns.'

'Big. That's good. Go on, Aleck. What is it?'

'Coal. The new mines. Cannel. I mean to put in ten

thousand. Ground floor. When we organise, we'll get three shares for one.'

'By George but it sounds good, Aleck' Then the shares will be worth – how much? And when?'

'About a year. They'll pay ten per cent half-yearly, and be worth thirty thousand. I know all about it; the advertisement is in the Cincinnati paper here.'

'Land, thirty thousand for ten – in a year! Let's jam in the whole capital and pull out ninety! I'll write and subscribe right now – tomorrow it may be too late.'

He was flying to the writing desk, but Aleck stopped him and put him back in his chair. She said: 'Don't lose your head so. We mustn't subscribe till we've got the money; don't you know that?'

Sally's excitement went down a degree or two, but he was not wholly appeased.

'Why, Aleck, we'll *have* it, you know – and so soon, too. He's probably out of his troubles before this, it's a hundred to nothing he's selecting his brimstone-shovel this very minute. Now, I think—'

Aleck shuddered, and said: 'How *can* you, Sally! Don't talk in that way, it is perfectly scandalous.'

'Oh, well, make it a halo, if you like, *I* don't care for his outfit, I was only just talking. Can't you let a person talk?'

'But why should you *want* to talk in that dreadful way? How would you like to have people talk so about *you*, and you not cold yet?'

'Nor likely to be for *one* while, I reckon, if my last act was giving away money for the sake of doing somebody a harm with it. But never mind about Tilbury, Aleck, let's talk about something worldly. It does seem to me that that mine is the place for the whole thirty. What's the objection?'

'All the eggs in one basket – that's the objection.'

'All right, if you say so. What about the other twenty? What do you mean to do with that?'

'There is no hurry; I am going to look around before I do anything with it.'

'All right, if your mind's made up,' sighed Sally. He was deep in thought a while, then he said: 'There'll be twenty thousand profit coming from the ten a year from now. We can spend that, can't we, Aleck?'

Aleck shook her head.

'No, dear,' she said, 'it won't sell high till we've had the first semi-annual dividend. You can spend part of that.'

'Shucks, only that – and a whole year to wait! Confound it, I—'

'Oh, do be patient! It might even be declared in three months – it's quite within the possibilities.'

'Oh, jolly! Oh, thanks!' and Sally jumped up and kissed his wife in gratitude. 'It'll be three thousand – three whole thousand! How much of it can we spend, Aleck? Make it liberal – do, dear, that's a good fellow.'

Aleck was pleased; so pleased that she yielded to the pressure and conceded a sum which her judgement told her was a foolish extravagance – a thousand dollars. Sally kissed her half a dozen times and even in that way could not express all his joy and thankfulness. This new access of gratitude and affection carried Aleck quite beyond the bounds of prudence, and before she could restrain herself she had made her darling another grant – a couple of thousand out of the fifty or sixty which she meant to clear within a year out of the twenty which still remained of the bequest. The happy tears sprang to Sally's eyes, and he said: 'Oh, I want to hug you!' And he did it. Then he got his notes and sat down and began to check off, for first purchase, the luxuries which he should earliest wish to secure. 'Horse – buggy – cutter – lap-robe – patent-leathers – dog – plug hat – church-pew – stem-winder – new teeth – *say*, Aleck!'

'Well?'

'Ciphering away, aren't you? That's right. Have you got the twenty thousand invested yet?'

'No, there's no hurry about that; I must look around first, and think.'

'But you are ciphering; what's it about?'

'Why, I have to find work for the thirty thousand that comes out of the coal, haven't I?'

'Scott, what a head! I never thought of that. How are you getting along? Where have you arrived?'

'Not very far – two years or three. I've turned it over twice; once in oil and once in wheat.'

'Why, Aleck, it's splendid! How does it aggregate?'

'I think – well, to be on the safe side, about a hundred and eighty thousand clear, though it will probably be more.'

'My! Isn't it wonderful? By gracious, luck has come our way at last, after all the hard sledding. Aleck!'

'Well?'

'I'm going to cash in a whole three hundred on the missionaries – what real right have we to care for expenses!'

'You couldn't do a nobler thing, dear; and it's just like your generous nature, you unselfish boy.'

The praise made Sally poignantly happy, but he was fair and just enough to say it was rightfully due to Aleck rather than to himself, since but for her he should never have had the money.

Then they went up to bed, and in their delirium of bliss

they forgot and left the candle burning in the parlour. They did not remember until they were undressed; then Sally was for letting it burn; he said they could afford it, if it was a thousand. But Aleck went down and put it out. A good job, too; for on her way back she hit on a scheme that would turn the hundred and eighty thousand into half a million before it had had time to get cold.

3

The little newspaper which Aleck had subscribed for was a Thursday sheet; it would make the trip of five hundred miles from Tilbury's village and arrive on Saturday. Tilbury's letter had started on Friday, more than a day too late for the benefactor to die and get into that week's issue, but in plenty of time to make connection for the next output. Thus the Fosters had to wait almost a complete week to find out whether anything of a satisfactory nature had happened to him or not. It was a long, long week, and the strain was a heavy one. The pair could hardly have borne it if their minds had not had the relief of wholesome diversion. We have seen that they had that. The woman was piling up fortunes right along, the man was spending them – spending all his wife would give him a chance at, at any rate.

At last the Saturday came, and the *Weekly Sagamore* arrived. Mrs Eversly Bennett was present. She was the Presbyterian parson's wife, and was working the Fosters for a charity. Talk now died a sudden death on the Foster side. Mrs Bennett presently discovered that her hosts were not hearing a word she was saying, so she got up, wondering and indignant, and went away. The moment she was out of the house, Aleck eagerly tore the wrapper from the paper, and her eyes and Sally's swept the columns for the death notices. Disappointment! Tilbury was not anywhere mentioned. Aleck was a Christian from the cradle, and duty and the force of habit required her to go through the motions. She pulled herself together and said, with a pious two-per-cent trade joyousness: 'Let us be humbly thankful that he has been spared; and—'

'Damn his treacherous hide, I wish—'

'Sally! For shame!'

'I don't care!' retorted the angry man. 'It's the way *you* feel, and if you weren't so immorally pious you'd be honest and say so.'

Aleck said, with wounded dignity: 'I do not see how you can say such unkind and unjust things. There is no such thing as immoral piety.'

Sally felt a pang, but tried to conceal it under a shuffling attempt to save his case by changing the form of it – as if changing the form while retaining the juice could deceive the expert he was trying to placate. He said: 'I didn't mean so bad as that, Aleck; I didn't really mean immoral piety, I only meant – meant – well, conventional piety, you know; er – shop piety; the – the – why, *you* know what I mean, Aleck – the – well, where you put up the plated article and play it for solid, you know, without intending anything improper, but just out of trade habit, ancient policy, petrified custom, loyalty to – to – hang it, I can't find the right words, but *you* know what I mean, Aleck, and that there isn't any harm in it. I'll try again. You see, it's this way. If a person—'

'You have said quite enough,' said Aleck, coldly; 'let the subject be dropped.'

'*I'm* willing,' fervently responded Sally, wiping the sweat from his forehead and looking the thankfulness he had no words for. Then, musingly, he apologised to himself. "I certainly held threes – I *know* it – but I drew and didn't fill. That's where I'm so often weak in the game. If I had stood pat – but I didn't. I never do. I don't know enough.'

Confessedly defeated, he was properly tame now and subdued. Aleck forgave him with her eyes.

The grand interest, the supreme interest, came instantly to the front again; nothing could keep it in the background many minutes on a stretch. The couple took up the puzzle of the absence of Tilbury's death notice. They discussed it every which way, more or less hopefully, but they had to finish where they began, and concede that the only really sane explanation of the absence of the notice must be – and without doubt was – that Tilbury was not dead. There was something sad about it, something even a little unfair, maybe, but there it was, and had to be put up with. They were agreed as to that. To Sally it seemed a strangely inscrutable dispensation; more inscrutable than usual he thought; one of the most unnecessarily inscrutable he could call to mind, in fact – and said so, with some feeling; but if he was hoping to draw Aleck he failed; she reserved her opinion, if she had one; she had not the habit of taking injudicious risks in any market, worldly or other.

The pair must wait for next week's paper – Tilbury had evidently postponed. That was their thought and their decision. So they put the subject away, and went about their affairs again, with as good heart as they could.

Now, if they had but known it, they had been wronging Tilbury all the time. Tilbury had kept faith, kept it to the letter; he was dead, he had died to schedule. He was dead more than four days now and used to it; entirely dead, perfectly dead, as dead as any other new person in the cemetery; dead in abundant time to get into that week's *Sagamore*, too, and only shut out by an accident; an accident which could not happen to a metropolitan journal, but which happens easily to a poor little village rag like the *Sagamore*. On this occasion, just as the editorial page was being locked up, a gratis quart of strawberry water-ice arrived from Hostetter's Ladies' and Gents' Ice Cream Parlours, and the stickful of rather chilly regret over Tilbury's translation got crowded out to make room for the editor's frantic gratitude.

On its way to the standing-galley Tilbury's notice got pied. Otherwise it would have gone into some future edition, for weekly *Sagamores* do not waste 'live' matter, and in their galleys 'live' matter is immortal, unless a pi accident intervene. But a thing that gets pied is dead, and for such there is no resurrection; its chance of seeing print is gone, forever and ever. And so, let Tilbury like it or not, let him rave in his grave to his fill, no matter – no mention of his death would ever see the light in the *Weekly Sagamore*.

4

Five weeks drifted tediously along. The *Sagamore* arrived regularly on the Saturdays, but never once contained a mention of Tilbury Foster. Sally's patience broke down at this point, and he said, resentfully: 'Damn his livers, he's immortal!'

Aleck gave him a very severe rebuke, and added, with icy solemnity: 'How would you feel if you were suddenly cut off just after such an awful remark had escaped out of you?'

Without sufficient reflection Sally responded: 'I'd feel I was lucky I hadn't got caught with it *in* me.'

Pride had forced him to say something, and as he could not think of any rational thing to say he flung that out. Then he stole a base – as he called it – that is, slipped from the presence, to keep from getting brayed in his wife's discussion-mortar.

Six months came and went. The *Sagamore* was still silent about Tilbury. Meantime Sally had several times thrown out a feeler – that is, a hint that he would like to know. Aleck had ignored the hints. Sally now resolved to brace up and risk a frontal attack. So he squarely proposed to disguise himself and go to Tilbury's village and surreptitiously find out as to the prospects. Aleck put her foot on the dangerous project with energy and decision. She said: 'What can you be thinking of? You do keep my hands full! You have to be watched all the time, like a little child, to keep you from walking into the fire. You'll stay right where you are.'

'Why, Aleck, I could do it and not be found out – I'm certain of it.'

'Sally Foster, don't you know you would have to inquire around?'

'Of course, but what of it? Nobody would suspect who I was.'

'Oh, listen to the man! Some day you've got to prove to the executors that you never inquired. What then?'

He had forgotten that detail. He didn't reply; there wasn't anything to say. Aleck added: 'Now then drop that notion out of your mind, and don't ever meddle with it again. Tilbury set that trap for you. Don't you know it's a trap? He is on the watch, and fully expecting you to blunder into it. Well, he is going to be disappointed – at least while I am on deck. Sally!'

'Well?'

'As long as you live, if it's a hundred years, don't you ever make an inquiry. Promise!'

'All right,' with a sigh and reluctantly.

Then Aleck softened and said: 'Don't be impatient. We are prospering; we can wait; there is no hurry. Our small dead-certain income increases all the time; and as to futures, I have not made a mistake yet – they are piling up by the thousands and the tens of thousands. There is not another family in the state with such prospects as ours. Already we are beginning to roll in eventual wealth. You know that, don't you?'

'Yes, Aleck, it's certainly so.'

'Then be grateful for what God is doing for us, and stop worrying. You do not believe we could have achieved these prodigious results without His special help and guidance, do you?'

Hesitatingly, 'N-no, I suppose not.' Then, with feeling and admiration, 'And yet, when it comes to judiciousness in watering a stock or putting up a hand to skin Wall Street, I don't give in that *you* need any outside amateur help, if I do I wish I—'

'Oh, *do* shut up! I know you do not mean any harm or any irreverence, poor boy, but you can't seem to open your mouth without letting out things to make a person shudder. You keep me in constant dread. For you and for all of us. Once I had no fear of the thunder, but now when I hear it I—'

Her voice broke and she began to cry, and could not finish. The sight of this smote Sally to the heart, and he took her in his arms and petted her and comforted her and promised better conduct, and upbraided himself and remorsefully pleaded for forgiveness. And he was in earnest, and sorry for what he had done and ready for any sacrifice that could make up for it.

And so, in privacy he thought long and deeply over the matter, resolving to do what should seem best. It was easy to *promise* reform; indeed he had already promised it. But would that do any real good, any permanent good? No, it would be but temporary – he knew his weakness, and confessed it to himself with sorrow – he could not keep the promise. Something surer and better must be devised, and he devised it. At cost of precious money which he had long been saving up, shilling by shilling, he put a lightning-rod on the house.

At a subsequent time he relapsed.

What miracles habit can do! And how quickly and how easily habits are acquired – both trifling habits and habits which profoundly change us. If by accident we wake at two in the morning a couple of nights in succession, we have need to be uneasy, for another repetition can turn the accident into a habit; and a month's dallying with whisky – but we all know these commonplace facts.

The castle-building habit, the daydreaming habit – how it grows! What a luxury it becomes; how we fly to its enchantments at every idle moment, how we revel in them, steep our souls in them, intoxicate ourselves with their beguiling fantasies – oh, yes, and how soon and how easily our dream-life and our material life become so intermingled and so fused together that we can't quite tell which is which anymore. By and by Aleck subscribed for a Chicago daily and for the *Wall Street Pointer*. With an eye single to finance she studied these as diligently all the week as she studied her Bible Sundays. Sally was lost in admiration, to note with what swift and sure strides her genius and judgement developed and expanded, in the forecasting and handling of the securities of both the material and spiritual markets. He was proud of her nerve and daring in exploiting worldly stocks, and just as proud of her conservative caution in working her spiritual deals. He noted that she never lost her head in either case; that with a splendid courage she often went short on worldly futures, but heedfully drew the line there – she was always long on the others. Her policy was quite sane and simple, as she explained it to him: what she put into earthly futures was for speculation, what she put into spiritual futures was for investment; she was willing to go into the one on a margin, and take chances, but in the case of the other, 'margin her no margins' – she wanted to cash in a hundred cents per dollar's worth and have the stock transferred on the books.

It took but a very few months to educate Aleck's imagination and Sally's. Each day's training added some-thing to the spread and effectiveness of the two machines. As a consequence, Aleck made imaginary money much faster than at first she had dreamed of making it, and Sally's competency in spending the overflow of it kept pace with the strain put upon it, right along. In the beginning Aleck had given the coal speculation a twelvemonth in which to materialise, and had been loath to grant that this term might possibly be shortened by nine months. But that was the feeble work, the nursery work, of a financial fancy that had had no teaching, no experience, no practice. These aids soon came, then that nine months vanished, and the imaginary ten-thousand-dollar investment came marching home with three hundred per cent profit on its back!

It was a great day for the pair of Fosters. They were speechless for joy. Also speechless for another reason: after much watching of the market, Aleck had lately, with fear and trembling, made her first flyer on a 'margin', using the remaining twenty thousand of the bequest in this risk. In her mind's eye she had seen it climb, point by point – always with a chance that the market would break – until at last her anxieties were too great for further endurance – she being new to the margin business and unhardened, as yet – and she gave her imaginary broker an imaginary order by imaginary telegraph to sell. She said forty thousand dollars profit was enough. The sale was made on the very day that the coal venture had returned with its rich freight. As I have said, the couple were speechless. They sat dazed and blissful, that night, trying to realise the immense fact, the overwhelming fact, that they were actually worth a hundred thousand dollars in clean imaginary cash. Yet so it was.

It was the last time that ever Aleck was afraid of a margin; at least afraid enough to let it break her sleep and pale her cheek to the extent that this first experience in that line had done.

Indeed it was a memorable night. Gradually the realisation that they were rich sank securely home into the souls of the pair, then they began to place the money. If we could have looked out through the eyes of these dreamers, we should have seen their tidy little wooden house disappear, and a two-storey brick with a cast-iron fence in front of it take its place; we should have seen a three-globed gas-chandelier grow down from the parlour ceiling; we should have seen the homely rag carpet turn to noble Brussels, a dollar and a half a yard; we should have seen the plebeian fireplace vanish away and a recherché big base-burner with isinglass windows take position and spread awe around. And we should have seen other things, too; among them the buggy, the lap-robe, the stovepipe hat, and so on.

From that time forth, although the daughters and the neighbours saw only the same old wooden house there, it was a two-storey brick to Aleck and Sally; and not a night went by that Aleck did not worry about the imaginary gas bills, and get for all comfort Sally's reckless retort, 'What of it? We can afford it.'

Before the couple went to bed, that first night that they were rich, they had decided that they must celebrate. They must give a party – that was the idea. But how to explain it – to the daughters and the neighbours? They could not expose the fact that they were rich. Sally was willing, even anxious, to do it; but Aleck kept her head and would not allow it. She said that although the money was as good as in, it would be as well to wait until it was actually in. On that policy she took her stand, and would not budge. The great secret must be kept, she said – kept from the daughters and everybody else.

The pair were puzzled. They must celebrate, they were determined to celebrate, but since the secret must be kept, what could they celebrate? No birthdays were due for three months. Tilbury wasn't available, evidently he was going to live forever; what the nation *could* they celebrate? That was Sally's way of putting it; and he was getting impatient, too, and harassed. But at last he hit it – just by sheer inspiration, as it seemed to him – and all their troubles were gone in a moment; they would celebrate the Discovery of America. A splendid idea!

Aleck was almost too proud of Sally for words – she said

she never would have thought of it. But Sally, although he was bursting with delight in the compliment and with wonder at himself, tried not to let on, and said it wasn't really anything, anybody could have done it. Whereat Aleck, with a prideful toss of her happy head, said: 'Oh, certainly! Anybody could – oh, anybody! Hosannah Dilkins, for instance! Or maybe Adelbert Peanut – oh, *dear* – yes! Well, I'd like to see them try it, that's all. Dear-me-suz, if they could think of the discovery of a forty-acre island it's more than I believe they could; and as for a whole continent, why, Sally Foster, you know perfectly well it would strain the livers and lights out of them and *then* they couldn't!'

The dear woman, she knew he had talent; and if affection made her overestimate the size of it a little, surely it was a sweet and gentle crime, and forgivable for its source's sake.

5

The celebration went off well. The friends were all present, both the young and the old. Among the young were Flossie and Gracie Peanut and their brother Adelbert, who was a rising young journeyman tinner, also Hosannah Dilkins, Jr, journeyman plasterer, just out of his apprenticeship. For many months Adelbert and Hosannah had been showing interest in Gwendolen and Clytemnestra Foster, and the parents of the girls had noticed this with private satisfaction. But they suddenly realised now that that feeling had passed. They recognised that the changed financial conditions had raised up a social bar between their daughters and the young mechanics. The daughters could now look higher – and must. Yes, must. They need marry nothing below the grade of lawyer or merchant; poppa and momma would take care of this; there must be no *mésalliances*.

However, these thinkings and projects of theirs were private, and did not show on the surface, and therefore threw no shadow upon the celebration. What showed upon the surface was a serene and lofty contentment and a dignity of carriage and gravity of deportment which compelled the admiration and likewise the wonder of the company. All noticed it, all commented upon it, but none was able to divine the secret of it. It was a marvel and a mystery. Three several persons remarked, without suspecting what clever shots they were making: 'It's as if they'd come into property.'

That was just it, indeed.

Most mothers would have taken hold of the matrimonial matter in the old regulation way; they would have given the girls a talking to, of a solemn sort and untactful – a lecture calculated to defeat its own purpose by producing tears and secret rebellion; and the said mothers would have further damaged the business by requesting the young mechanics to discontinue their attentions. But this mother was different. She was practical. She said nothing to any of the young people concerned, nor to anyone else except Sally. He listened to her and understood; understood and admired. He said: 'I get the idea. Instead of finding fault with the samples on view, thus hurting feelings and obstructing trade without occasion, you merely offer a higher class of goods for the money, and leave nature to take her course. It's wisdom, Aleck, solid wisdom, and sound as a nut. Who's your fish? Have you nominated him yet?'

No, she hadn't. They must look the market over – which

they did. To start with, they considered and discussed Bradish, rising young lawyer, and Fulton, rising young dentist. Sally must invite them to dinner. But not right away; there was no hurry, Aleck said. Keep an eye on the pair, and wait; nothing would be lost by going slowly in so important a matter.

It turned out that this was wisdom, too; for inside of three weeks Aleck made a wonderful strike which swelled her imaginary hundred thousand to four hundred thousand of the same quality. She and Sally were in the clouds that evening. For the first time they introduced champagne at dinner. Not real champagne, but plenty real enough for the amount of imagination expended on it. It was Sally that did it, and Aleck weakly submitted. At bottom both were troubled and ashamed, for he was a high-up Son of Temperance, and at funerals wore an apron which no dog could look upon and retain his reason and his opinion; and she was a W.C.T.U., with all that that implies of boiler-iron virtue and unendurable holiness. But there it was: the pride of riches was beginning its disintegrating work. They had lived to prove, once more, a sad truth which had been proven many times before in the world: that whereas principle is a great and noble protection against showy and degrading vanities and vices, poverty is worth six of it. More than four hundred thousand dollars to the good! They took up the matrimonial matter again. Neither the dentist nor the lawyer was mentioned; there was no occasion; they were out of the running. Disqualified. They discussed the son of the pork-packer and the son of the village banker. But finally, as in the previous case, they concluded to wait and think, and go cautiously and sure.

Luck came their way again. Aleck, ever watchful, saw a

great and risky chance, and took a daring flyer. A time of trembling, of doubt, of awful uneasiness followed, for non-success meant absolute ruin and nothing short of it. Then came the result, and Aleck, faint with joy, could hardly control her voice when she said: 'The suspense is over, Sally – and we are worth a cold million!'

Sally wept for gratitude, and said: 'Oh, Electra, jewel of women, darling of my heart, we are free at last, we roll in wealth, we need never scrimp again. It's a case for Veuve Clicquot!' and he got out a pint of spruce beer and made sacrifice, he saying 'Damn the expense,' and she rebuking him gently with reproachful but humid and happy eyes.

They shelved the pork-packer's son and the banker's son, and sat down to consider the Governor's son and the son of the Congressman.

6

It were a weariness to follow in detail the leaps and bounds the Foster fictitious finances took from this time forth. It was marvellous, it was dizzying, it was dazzling. Everything Aleck touched turned to fairy gold, and heaped itself glittering toward the firmament. Millions upon millions poured in, and still the mighty stream flowed thundering along, still its vast volume increased. Five millions – ten millions – twenty – thirty – was there never to be an end?

Two years swept by in a splendid delirium, the in-toxicated Fosters scarcely noticing the flight of time. They were now worth three hundred million dollars; they were in every board of directors of every prodigious combine in the country; and still, as time drifted along, the millions went on piling up, five at a time, ten at a time, as fast as they could tally them off, almost. The three hundred doubled itself – then doubled again – and yet again – and yet once more!

Twenty-four hundred millions!

The business was getting a little confused. It was necessary to take an account of stock, and straighten it out. The Fosters knew it, they felt it, they realised that it was imperative; but they also knew that to do it properly and perfectly the task must be carried to a finish without a break when once it was begun. A ten-hour job; and where could *they* find ten leisure hours in a bunch? Sally was selling pins and sugar and calico all day and everyday; Aleck was cooking and washing dishes and sweeping and making beds all day and everyday, with none to help, for the daughters were being saved up for high society. The Fosters knew there was one way to get the ten hours, and only one. Both were ashamed to name it; each waited for the other to do it. Finally Sally said: 'Somebody's got to give in. It's up to me. Consider that I've named it – never mind pronouncing it out loud.'

Aleck coloured, but was grateful. Without further remark, they fell. Fell, and broke the Sabbath. For that was their only free ten-hour stretch. It was but another step in the downward path. Others would follow. Vast wealth has temptations which fatally and surely undermine the moral structure of persons not habituated to its possession.

They pulled down the shades and broke the Sabbath. With hard and patient labour they overhauled their holdings, and listed them. And a long-drawn procession of formidable names it was! Starting with the Railway Systems, Steamer Lines, Standard Oil, Ocean Cables, Diluted Telegraph, and all the rest, and winding up with

Klondike, De Beers, Tammany Graft, and Shady Privileges in the Post-office Department.

Twenty-four hundred millions, and all safely planted in Good Things, gilt-edged and interest-bearing. Income, $120,000,000 a year. Aleck fetched a long purr of soft delight, and said: 'Is it enough?'

'It is, Aleck.'

'What shall we do?'

'Stand pat.'

'Retire from business?'

'That's it.'

'I am agreed. The good work is finished; we will take a long rest and enjoy the money.'

'Good! Aleck?'

'Yes, dear?'

'How much of the income can we spend?'

'The whole of it.'

It seemed to her husband that a ton of chains fell from his limbs. He did not say a word; he was happy beyond the power of speech.

After that, they broke the Sabbaths right along, as fast as they turned up. It is the first wrong steps that count. Every Sunday they put in the whole day, after morning service, on inventions – inventions of ways to spend the money. They got to continuing this delicious dissipation until past midnight; and at every seance Aleck lavished millions upon great charities and religious enterprises, and Sally lavished like sums upon matters to which (at first) he gave definite names. Only at first. Later the names gradually lost sharpness of outline, and eventually faded into 'sundries', thus becoming entirely – but safely – undescriptive. For Sally was crumbling. The placing of these millions added seriously and most uncomfortably to the family expenses – in tallow candles. For a while Aleck was worried. Then, after a little, she ceased to worry, for the occasion of it was gone. She was pained, she was grieved, she was ashamed; but she said nothing, and so became an accessory. Sally was taking candles; he was robbing the store. It is ever thus. Vast wealth, to the person unaccustomed to it, is a bane; it eats into the flesh and bone of his morals. When the Fosters were poor, they could have been trusted with untold candles. But now they – but let us not dwell upon it. From candles to apples is but a step: Sally got to taking apples; then soap; then maple sugar; then canned goods; then crockery. How easy it is to go from bad to worse, when once we have started upon a downward course!

Meantime, other effects had been milestoning the course of the Fosters' splendid financial march. The fictitious brick dwelling had given place to an imaginary granite one with a chequerboard mansard roof; in time this one disappeared and gave place to a still grander home – and so on and so on. Mansion after mansion, made of air, rose, higher, broader, finer, and each in its turn vanished away; until now, in these latter great days, our dreamers were in fancy housed, in a distant region, in a sumptuous vast palace which looked out from a leafy summit upon a noble prospect of vale and river and receding hills steeped in tinted mists – and all private, all the property of the dreamers; a palace swarming with liveried servants, and populous with guests of fame and power, hailing from all the world's capitals, foreign and domestic.

This palace was far, far away toward the rising sun, immeasurably remote, astronomically remote, in Newport, Rhode Island, Holy Land of High Society, ineffable

Domain of the American Aristocracy. As a rule, they spent a part of every Sabbath – after morning service – in this sumptuous home, the rest of it they spent in Europe, or in dawdling around in their private yacht. Six days of sordid and plodding fact-life at home on the ragged edge of Lakeside and straitened means, the seventh in Fairyland – such had become their programme and their habit.

In their sternly restricted fact-life they remained as of old – plodding, diligent, careful, practical, economical. They stuck loyally to the little Presbyterian Church, and laboured faithfully in its interests and stood by its high and tough doctrines with all their mental and spiritual energies. But in their dream-life they obeyed the invitations of their fancies, whatever they might be, and howsoever the fancies might change. Aleck's fancies were not very capricious, and not frequent, but Sally's scattered a good deal. Aleck, in her dream-life, went over to the Episcopal camp, on account of its large official titles; next she became High-church on account of the candles and shows; and next she naturally changed to Rome, where there were cardinals and more candles. But these excursions were as nothing to Sally's. His dream-life was a glowing and continuous and persistent excitement, and he kept every part of it fresh and sparkling by frequent changes, the religious part along with the rest. He worked his religions hard, and changed them with his shirt.

The liberal spendings of the Fosters upon their fancies began early in their prosperities, and grew in prodigality step by step with their advancing fortunes. In time they became truly enormous. Aleck built a university or two per Sunday; also a hospital or two; also a Rowton hotel or so; also a batch of churches; now and then a cathedral;

and once, with untimely and ill-chosen playfulness, Sally said, 'It was a cold day when she didn't ship a cargo of missionaries to persuade unreflecting Chinamen to trade off twenty-four carat Confucianism for counterfeit Christianity.'

This rude and unfeeling language hurt Aleck to the heart, and she went from the presence crying. That spectacle went to his own heart, and in his pain and shame he would have given worlds to have those unkind words back. She had uttered no syllable of reproach – and that cut him. Not one suggestion that he look at his own record – and she could have made, oh, so many, and such blistering ones! Her generous silence brought a swift revenge, for it turned his thoughts upon himself, it summoned before him a spectral procession, a moving vision of his life as he had been leading it these past few years of limitless prosperity, and as he sat there reviewing it his cheeks burned and his soul was steeped in humiliation. Look at her life – how fair it was, and tending ever upward and look at his own – how frivolous, how charged with mean vanities, how selfish, how empty, how ignoble! And its trend – never upward, but downward, ever downward!

He instituted comparisons between her record and his own. He had found fault with her – so he mused – *he*! And what could he say for himself? When she built her first church what was he doing? Gathering other blasé multi-millionaires into a Poker Club; defiling his own palace with it; losing hundreds of thousands to it at every sitting, and sillily vain of the admiring notoriety it made for him. When she was building her first university, what was he doing? Polluting himself with a gay and dissipated secret life in the company of other fast bloods, multimillionaires in money and paupers in character. When she was building her first foundling asylum, what was he doing? Alas! When she was projecting her noble Society for the Purifying of the Sex, what was he doing? Ah, what, indeed! When she and the W.C.T.U. and the Woman with the Hatchet, moving with resistless march, were sweeping the fatal bottle from the land, what was he doing? Getting drunk three times a day. When she, builder of a hundred cathedrals, was being gratefully welcomed and blest in papal Rome and decorated with the Golden Rose which she had so honourably earned, what was he doing? Breaking the bank at Monte Carlo.

He stopped. He could go no farther; he could not bear the rest. He rose up, with a great resolution upon his lips: this secret life should be revealed, and confessed; no longer would he live it clandestinely; he would go and tell her All.

And that is what he did. He told her All; and wept upon her bosom; wept, and moaned, and begged for her forgiveness. It was a profound shock, and she staggered under the blow, but he was her own, the core of her heart, the blessing of her eyes, her all in all, she could deny him nothing, and she forgave him. She felt that he could never again be quite to her what he had been before; she knew that he could only repent, and not reform; yet all morally defaced and decayed as he was, was he not her own, her very own, the idol of her deathless worship? She said she was his serf, his slave, and she opened her yearning heart and took him in.

7

One Sunday afternoon sometime after this they were sailing the summer seas in their dream-yacht, and reclining in lazy luxury under the awning of the afterdeck. There was silence, for each was busy with his own thoughts. These seasons of silence had insensibly been growing more and more frequent of late; the old nearness and cordiality were waning. Sally's terrible revelation had done its work; Aleck had tried hard to drive the memory of it out of her mind, but it would not go, and the shame and bitterness of it were poisoning her gracious dream-life. She could see now (on Sundays) that her husband was becoming a bloated and repulsive Thing. She could not close her eyes to this, and in these days she no longer looked at him, Sundays, when she could help it.

But she – was she herself without blemish? Alas, she knew she was not. She was keeping a secret from him, she was acting dishonourably toward him, and many a pang it was costing her. She was breaking the compact, and concealing it from him. Under strong temptation she had gone into business again; she had risked their whole fortune in a purchase of all the railway systems and coal and steel companies in the country on a margin, and she was now trembling, every Sabbath hour, lest through some chance word of hers he find it out. In her misery and remorse for this treachery she could not keep her heart from going out to him in pity; she was filled with compunctions to see him lying there, drunk and content, and never suspecting. Never suspecting – trusting her with a perfect and pathetic trust, and she holding over him by a thread a possible calamity of so devastating a—

'*Say* – Aleck!'

The interrupting words brought her suddenly to herself. She was grateful to have that persecuting subject from her thoughts, and she answered, with much of the old-time tenderness in her tone: 'Yes, dear.'

'Do you know, Aleck, I think we are making a mistake – that is, you are. I mean about the marriage business.' He sat up, fat and froggy and benevolent, like a bronze Buddha, and grew earnest. 'Consider – it's more than five years. You've continued the same policy from the start: with every rise, always holding on for five points higher. Always when I think we are going to have some weddings, you see a bigger thing ahead, and I undergo another disappointment. I think you are too hard to please. Someday we'll get left. First, we turned down the dentist and the lawyer. That was all right – it was sound. Next, we turned down the banker's son and the pork-butcher's heir – right again, and sound. Next, we turned down the Congressman's son and the Governor's – right as a trivet, I confess it. Next, the Senator's son and the son of the Vice-President of the United States – perfectly right, there's no permanency about those little distinctions. Then you went for the aristocracy, and I thought we had struck oil at last – yes. We would make a plunge at the Four Hundred, and pull in some ancient lineage, venerable, holy, ineffable, mellow with the antiquity of a hundred and fifty years, disinfected of the ancestral odours of salt cod and pelts all of a century ago, and unsmirched by a day's work since, and then! why, then the marriages, of course. But no, along comes a pair of real aristocrats from Europe, and straightway you throw over the half-breeds. It was awfully discouraging, Aleck! Since then, what a procession! You turned down the baronets for a pair of barons, you turned down the barons for a pair of viscounts; the viscounts for a pair of earls; the earls for a pair of marquises; the marquises for a brace of dukes. *Now*, Aleck, cash in! – you've played the limit. You've got a job lot of four dukes under the hammer, of four nationalities; all sound in wind and limb and pedigree, all bankrupt and in debt up to the ears. They come high, but we can afford it. Come, Aleck, don't delay any longer, don't keep up the suspense: take the whole layout, and leave the girls to choose!'

Aleck had been smiling blandly and contentedly all through this arraignment of her marriage policy; a pleasant light, as of triumph with perhaps a nice surprise peeping out through it, rose in her eyes, and she said, as calmly as she could: 'Sally, what would you say to – *royalty*?'

Prodigious! Poor man, it knocked him silly, and he fell over the garboard strake and barked his shin on the cat-heads. He was dizzy for a moment, then he gathered himself up and limped over and sat down by his wife and beamed his old-time admiration and affection upon her in floods, out of his bleary eyes.

'By George!' he said, fervently, 'Aleck, you *are* great – the greatest woman in the whole earth! I can't ever learn the whole size of you. I can't ever learn the immeasurable deeps of you. Here I've been considering myself qualified to criticise your game. *I!* Why, if I had stopped to think, I'd have known you had a lone hand up your sleeve. Now, dear heart, I'm all red-hot impatience – tell me about it!'

The flattered and happy woman put her lips to his ear and whispered a princely name. It made him catch his breath, it lit his face with exultation.

'Land!' he said, 'it's a stunning catch! He's got a gambling-hall, and a graveyard, and a bishop, and a cathedral – all his very own. And all gilt-edged five-hundred per cent stock, every detail of it; the tidiest little property in Europe. And that graveyard – it's the selectest in the world: none but suicides admitted; yes, sir, and the free-list suspended, too, *all* the time. There isn't much land in the principality, but there's enough: eight hundred acres in the graveyard and forty-two outside. It's a *sovereignty* – that's the main thing; *land's* nothing. There's plenty land, Sahara's drugged with it.'

Aleck glowed; she was profoundly happy. She said: 'Think of it, Sally – it is a family that has never married outside the Royal and Imperial Houses of Europe: our grandchildren will sit upon thrones!'

'True as you live, Aleck – and bear sceptres, too, and handle them as naturally and nonchalantly as I handle a yardstick. It's a grand catch, Aleck. He's corralled, is he? Can't get away? You didn't take him on a margin?'

'No. Trust me for that. He's not a liability, he's an asset. So is the other one.'

'Who is it, Aleck?'

'His Royal Highness Sigismund-Siegfried-Lauenfeld-Dinkelspiel-Schwartzenberg Blutwurst, Hereditary Grand Duke of Katzenyammer.'

'No! You can't mean it!'

'It's as true as I'm sitting here, I give you my word,' she answered.

His cup was full, and he hugged her to his heart with rapture, saying: 'How wonderful it all seems, and how beautiful! It's one of the oldest and noblest of the three hundred and sixty-four ancient German principalities, and one of the few that was allowed to retain its royal estate when Bismarck got done trimming them. I know that farm, I've been there. It's got a ropewalk and a candle factory and an army. Standing army. Infantry and cavalry. Three soldiers and a horse. Aleck, it's been a long wait, and full of heartbreak and hope deferred, but God knows I am happy now. Happy, and grateful to you, my own, who have done it all. When is it to be?'

'Next Sunday.'

'Good. And we'll want to do these weddings up in the very regalest style that's going. It's properly due to the royal quality of the parties of the first part. Now as I understand it, there is only one kind of marriage that is sacred to royalty, exclusive to royalty: it's the morganatic.'

'What do they call it that for, Sally?'

'I don't know, but anyway it's royal, and royal only.'

'Then we will insist upon it. More – I will compel it. It is morganatic marriage or none.'

'That settles it!' said Sally, rubbing his hands with delight. 'And it will be the very first in America. Aleck, it will make Newport sick.'

Then they fell silent, and drifted away upon their dream-wings to the far regions of the earth to invite all the crowned heads and their families and provide gratis transportation for them.

8

During three days the couple walked upon air, with their heads in the clouds. They were but vaguely conscious of their surroundings, they saw all things dimly, as through a veil, they were steeped in dreams, often they did not hear when they were spoken to, they often did not understand when they heard; they answered confusedly or at random; Sally sold molasses by weight, sugar by the yard, and furnished soap when asked for candles, and Aleck put the cat in the wash and fed milk to the soiled linen. Everybody was stunned and amazed, and went about muttering, 'What *can* be the matter with the Fosters?'

Three days. Then came events! Things had taken a happy turn, and for forty-eight hours Aleck's imaginary corner had been booming. Up – up – still up! Cost-point was passed. Still up – and up – and up! Five points above cost – then ten – fifteen – twenty! Twenty points cold profit on the vast venture, now, and Aleck's imaginary brokers were shouting frantically by imaginary long-distance, 'Sell! sell! for Heaven's sake *sell*!'

She broke the splendid news to Sally, and he, too, said 'Sell! Sell – oh, don't make a blunder, now, you own the earth! – sell, sell!' But she set her iron will and lashed it amidships, and said she would hold on for five points more if she died for it.

It was a fatal resolve. The very next day came the historic crash, the record crash, the devastating crash, when the bottom fell out of Wall Street, and the whole body of gilt-edged stocks dropped ninety-five points in five hours, and the multimillionaire was seen begging his bread in the Bowery. Aleck sternly held her grip and 'put up' as long as she could, but at last there came a call which she was powerless to meet, and her imaginary brokers sold her out. Then, and not till then, the man in her was vanquished, and the woman in her resumed sway. She put her arm about her husband's neck and wept, saying—

'I am to blame, do not forgive me, I cannot bear it. We are paupers! Paupers, and I am so miserable. The weddings will never come off; all that is past; we could not even buy the dentist, now.'

A bitter reproach was on Sally's tongue: 'I *begged* you to sell, but you—'

He did not say it; he had not the heart to add a hurt to that broken and repentant spirit. A nobler thought came to him and he said: 'Bear up, my Aleck, all is not lost! You really never invested a penny of my uncle's bequest, but only its unmaterialised future; what we have lost was only the increment harvested from that future by your incomparable financial judgement and sagacity. Cheer up, banish these griefs; we still have the thirty thousand untouched; and with the experience which you have acquired, think what you will be able to do with it in a couple of years! The marriages are not off, they are only postponed.'

These were blessed words. Aleck saw how true they were, and their influence was electric; her tears ceased to flow, and her great spirit rose to its full stature again. With flashing eye and grateful heart, and with hand uplifted in pledge and prophecy, she said: 'Now and here I proclaim—'

But she was interrupted by a visitor. It was the editor and proprietor of the *Sagamore*. He had happened into Lakeside to pay a duty-call upon an obscure grandmother of his who was nearing the end of her pilgrimage, and with the idea of combining business with grief he had looked up the Fosters, who had been so absorbed in other things for the past four years that they had neglected to pay up their subscription. Six dollars due. No visitor could have been more welcome. He would know all about Uncle Tilbury and what his chances might be getting to be, cemetery-wards. They could of course ask no questions, for that would squelch the bequest, but they could nibble around on the edge of the subject and hope for results. The scheme did not work. The obtuse editor did not know he was being nibbled at; but at last chance accomplished what art had failed in. In illustration of something under discussion which required the help of metaphor, the editor said: 'Land, it's as tough as Tilbury Foster! – as *we* say.'

It was sudden, and it made the Fosters jump. The editor noticed it and said, apologetically: 'No harm intended, I assure you. It's just a saying; just a joke, you know – nothing in it. Relation of yours?'

Sally crowded his burning eagerness down, and answered with all the indifference he could assume: 'I – well, not that I know of, but we've heard of him.' The editor was thankful, and resumed his composure. Sally added, 'Is he – is he well?'

'Is he *well*! Why, bless you he's in Sheol these five years!'

'The Fosters were trembling with grief, though it felt like joy. Sally said, non-committally – and tentatively: 'Ah, well, such is life, and none can escape – not even the rich are spared.'

The editor laughed.

'If you are including Tilbury,' said he, 'it don't apply. *He* hadn't a cent; the town had to bury him.'

The Fosters sat petrified for two minutes; petrified and cold. Then, white-faced and weak-voiced, Sally asked: 'Is it true? Do you *know* it to be true?'

'Well, I should say! I was one of the executors. He hadn't anything to leave but a wheelbarrow, and he left that to me. It hadn't any wheel, and wasn't any good. Still, it was something, and so, to square up, I scribbled off a sort of a little obituarial send-off for him, but it got crowded out.'

The Fosters were not listening – their cup was full, it could contain no more. They sat with bowed heads, dead to all things but the ache at their hearts.

An hour later. Still they sat there, bowed, motionless, silent, the visitor long ago gone, they unaware.

Then they stirred, and lifted their heads wearily, and gazed at each other wistfully, dreamily, dazed, then presently began to twaddle to each other in a wandering and childish way. At intervals they lapsed into silences, leaving a sentence unfinished, seemingly either unaware of it or losing their way. Sometimes, when they woke out of these silences, they had a dim and transient consciousness that something had happened to their minds; then with a dumb and yearning solicitude they would softly caress each other's hands in mutual compassion and support, as if they would say: 'I am near you, I will not forsake you, we will bear it together; somewhere there is release and forgetfulness, somewhere there is a grave and peace; be patient, it will not be long.'

They lived yet two years, in mental night, always brooding, steeped in vague regrets and melancholy dreams, never speaking; then release came to both on the same day.

Toward the end the darkness lifted from Sally's ruined mind for a moment, and he said: 'Vast wealth, acquired by sudden and unwholesome means, is a snare. It did us no good, transient were its feverish pleasures; yet for its sake we threw away our sweet and simple and happy life – let others take warning by us.'

He lay silent a while, with closed eyes; then as the chill of death crept upward toward his heart, and consciousness was fading from his brain, he muttered: 'Money had brought him misery, and he took his revenge upon us, who had done him no harm. He had his desire: with base and cunning calculation he left us but thirty thousand, knowing we would try to increase it, and ruin our life and break our hearts. Without added expense he could have left us far above desire of increase, far above the temptation to speculate, and a kinder soul would have done it but in him was no generous spirit, no pity, no—'

A Californian's Tale

Thirty-five years ago I was out prospecting on the Stanislaus, tramping all day long with pick and pan and horn, and washing a hatful of dirt here and there, always expecting to make a rich strike, and never doing it. It was a lovely region, woodsy, balmy, delicious, and had once been populous long years before, but now the people had vanished and the charming paradise was a solitude. They went away when the surface diggings gave out. In one place, where a busy little city with banks and newspapers and fire companies and a mayor and aldermen had been, was nothing but a wide expanse of emerald turf, with not even the faintest sign that human life had ever been present there. This was down toward Turtletown. In the country neighbourhood thereabouts, along the dusty roads, one found at intervals the prettiest little cottage homes, snug and cosy, and so cobwebbed with vines snowed thick with roses that the doors and windows were wholly hidden from sight – sign that these were deserted homes, forsaken years ago by defeated and disappointed families who could neither sell them nor give them away. Now and then, half an hour apart, one came across solitary log cabins of the earliest mining days, built by the first gold miners, the predecessors of the cottage builders. In some few cases these cabins were still occupied; and when this was so, you could

depend upon it that the occupant was the very pioneer
who had built the cabin; and you could depend on another
thing, too – that he was there because he had once had his
opportunity to go home to the States rich, and had not
done it; had rather lost his wealth, and had then in his
humiliation resolved to sever all communication with his
home relatives and friends, and be to them thenceforth as
one dead. Round about California in that day were
scattered a host of these living dead men – pride-smitten
poor fellows, grizzled and old at forty, whose secret
thoughts were made all of regrets and longings – regrets
for their wasted lives, and longings to be out of the
struggle and done with it all.

It was a lonesome land! Not a sound in all those peaceful
expanses of grass and woods but the drowsy hum of insects;
no glimpse of man or beast; nothing to keep up your spirits
and make you glad to be alive. And so, at last, in the early
part of the afternoon, when I caught sight of a human
creature, I felt a most grateful uplift. This person was a
man about forty-five years old, and he was standing at the
gate of one of those cosy little roseclad cottages of the sort
already referred to. However, this one hadn't a deserted
look; it had the look of being lived in and petted and cared
for and looked after; and so had its front yard, which was a
garden of flowers, abundant, gay, and flourishing. I was
invited in, of course, and required to make myself at home –
it was the custom of the country.

It was delightful to be in such a place after long weeks of
daily and nightly familiarity with miners' cabins – with all
which this implies of dirt floor, never-made beds, tin plates
and cups, bacon and beans and black coffee, and nothing of
ornament but war pictures from the Eastern illustrated

papers tacked to the log walls. That was all hard, cheerless, materialistic desolation, but here was a nest which had aspects to rest the tired eye and refresh that something in one's nature which, after long fasting, recognises, when confronted by the belongings of art, howsoever cheap and modest they may be, that it has unconsciously been famishing and now has found nourishment. I could not have believed that a rag carpet could feast me so, and so content me; or that there could be such solace to the soul in wallpaper and framed lithographs, and bright-coloured tidies and lamp-mats, and Windsor chairs, and varnished whatnots, with seashells and books and china vases on them, and the score of little unclassifiable tricks and touches that a woman's hand distributes about a home, which one sees without knowing he sees them, yet would miss in a moment if they were taken away. The delight that was in my heart showed in my face, and the man saw it and was pleased; saw it so plainly that he answered it as if it had been spoken.

'All her work,' he said, caressingly; 'she did it all herself every bit,' and he took the room in with a glance which was full of affectionate worship. One of those soft Japanese fabrics with which women drape with careful negligence the upper part of a picture frame was out of adjustment. He noticed it, and rearranged it with cautious pains, stepping back several times to gauge the effect before he got it to suit him. Then he gave it a light finishing pat or two with his hand, and said: 'She always does that. You can't tell just what it lacks, but it does lack something until you've done that – you can see it yourself after it's done, but that is all you know; you can't find out the law of it. It's like the finishing pats a mother gives the child's hair after she's got it combed and brushed, I reckon. I've seen her fix all these things so much that I can do them all just her way, though I don't know the law of any of them. But she knows the law. She knows the why and the how both; but I don't know the why; I only know the how.'

He took me into a bedroom so that I might wash my hands; such a bedroom as I had not seen for years: white counterpane, white pillows, carpeted floor, papered walls, pictures, dressing table, with mirror and pincushion and dainty toilet things; and in the corner a washstand, with real china-ware bowl and pitcher, and with soap in a china dish, and on a rack more than a dozen towels – towels too clean and white for one out of practice to use without some vague sense of profanation. So my face spoke again, and he answered with gratified words: 'All her work; she did it all herself – every bit. Nothing here that hasn't felt the touch of her hand. Now you would think — But I mustn't talk so much.'

By this time I was wiping my hands and glancing from detail to detail of the room's belongings, as one is apt to do when he is in a new place, where everything he sees is a comfort to his eye and his spirit; and I became conscious, in one of those unaccountable ways, you know, that there was something there somewhere that the man wanted me to discover for myself. I knew it perfectly, and I knew he was trying to help me by furtive indications with his eye, so I tried hard to get on the right track, being eager to gratify him. I failed several times, as I could see out of the corner of my eye without being told; but at last I knew I must be looking straight at the thing – knew it from the pleasure issuing in invisible waves from him. He broke into a happy laugh, and rubbed his hands together, and cried out: 'That's it! You've found it. I knew you would. It's her picture.'

I went to the little black-walnut bracket on the farther wall, and did find there what I had not yet noticed – a daguerreotype-case. It contained the sweetest girlish face, and the most beautiful, as it seemed to me, that I had ever seen. The man drank the admiration from my face, and was fully satisfied.

'Nineteen her last birthday,' he said, as he put the picture back; 'and that was the day we were married. When you see her – ah, just wait till you see her!'

'Where is she? When will she be in?'

'Oh, she's away now. She's gone to see her people. They live forty or fifty miles from here. She's been gone two weeks today.'

'When do you expect her back?'

'This is Wednesday. She'll be back Saturday, in the evening – about nine o'clock, likely.'

I felt a sharp sense of disappointment.

'I'm sorry, because I'll be gone then,' I said, regretfully.

'Gone? No – why should you go? Don't go. She'll be so disappointed.'

She would be disappointed – that beautiful creature! If she had said the words herself they could hardly have blessed me more. I was feeling a deep, strong longing to see her – a longing so supplicating, so insistent, that it made me afraid. I said to myself: 'I will go straight away from this place, for my peace of mind's sake.'

'You see, she likes to have people come and stop with us – people who know things, and can talk – people like you. She delights in it; for she knows – oh, she knows nearly everything herself, and can talk, oh, like a bird – and the books she reads, why, you would be astonished. Don't go; it's only a little while, you know, and she'll be so disappointed.'

I heard the words, but hardly noticed them, I was so deep in my thinkings and strugglings. He left me, but I didn't know. Presently he was back with the picture case in his hand, and he held it open before me and said: 'There, now, tell her to her face you could have stayed to see her, and you wouldn't.'

That second glimpse broke down my good resolution. I would stay and take the risk. That night we smoked the tranquil pipe, and talked till late about various things, but mainly about her; and certainly I had had no such pleasant and restful time for many a day. The Thursday followed and slipped comfortably away. Toward twilight a big miner from three miles away came – one of the grizzled, stranded pioneers – and gave us warm salutation, clothed in grave and sober speech. Then he said: 'I only just dropped over to ask about the little madam, and when is she coming home. Any news from her?'

'Oh yes, a letter. Would you like to hear it, Tom?'

'Well, I should think I would, if you don't mind, Henry!'

Henry got the letter out of his wallet, and said he would skip some of the private phrases, if we were willing; then he went on and read the bulk of it – a loving, sedate, and altogether charming and gracious piece of handiwork, with a postscript full of affectionate regards and messages to Tom, and Joe, and Charley, and other close friends and neighbours.

As the reader finished, he glanced at Tom, and cried out: 'Oho, you're at it again! Take your hands away, and let me see your eyes. You always do that when I read a letter from her. I will write and tell her.'

'Oh no, you mustn't, Henry. I'm getting old, you know, and any little disappointment makes me want to cry. I thought she'd be here herself, and now you've got only a letter.'

'Well, now, what put that in your head? I thought everybody knew she wasn't coming till Saturday.'

'Saturday! Why, come to think, I did know it. I wonder what's the matter with me lately? Certainly I knew it. Ain't we all getting ready for her? Well, I must be going now. But I'll be on hand when she comes, old man!'

Late Friday afternoon another gray veteran tramped over from his cabin a mile or so away, and said the boys wanted to have a little gaiety and a good time Saturday night, if Henry thought she wouldn't be too tired after her journey to be kept up.

'Tired? She tired! Oh, hear the man! Joe, *you* know she'd sit up six weeks to please any one of you!'

When Joe heard that there was a letter, he asked to have it read, and the loving messages in it for him broke the old fellow all up; but he said he was such an old wreck that *that* would happen to him if she only just mentioned his name. 'Lord, we miss her so!' he said.

Saturday afternoon I found I was taking out my watch pretty often. Henry noticed it, and said, with a startled look: 'You don't think she ought to be here so soon, do you?'

I felt caught, and a little embarrassed; but I laughed, and said it was a habit of mine when I was in a state of expectancy. But he didn't seem quite satisfied, and from that time on he began to show uneasiness. Four times he walked me up the road to a point whence we could see a long distance; and there he would stand, shading his eyes with his hand, and looking. Several times he said: 'I'm getting worried, I'm getting right down worried. I know she's not due till about nine o'clock, and yet something seems to be trying to warn me that something's happened. You don't think anything has happened, do you?'

I began to get pretty thoroughly ashamed of him for his childishness; and at last, when he repeated that imploring question still another time, I lost my patience for the moment, and spoke pretty brutally to him. It seemed to shrivel him up and cow him; and he looked so wounded and so humble after that, that I detested myself for having done the cruel and unnecessary thing. And so I was glad when Charley, another veteran, arrived toward the edge of the evening, and nestled up to Henry to hear the letter read, and talked over the preparations for the welcome. Charley fetched out one hearty speech after another, and did his best to drive away his friend's bodings and apprehensions.

'Anything *happened* to her? Henry, that's pure nonsense. There isn't anything going to happen to her; just make your mind easy as to that. What did the letter say? Said she was well, didn't it? And said she'd be here by nine o'clock, didn't it? Did you ever know her to fail of her word? Why, you know you never did. Well, then, don't you fret; she'll *be* here, and that's absolutely certain, and as sure as you are born. Come, now, let's get to decorating – not much time left.'

Pretty soon Tom and Joe arrived, and then all hands set about adorning the house with flowers. Toward nine the three miners said that as they had brought their instruments they might as well tune up, for the boys and girls would soon be arriving now, and hungry for a good, old-fashioned break-down. A fiddle, a banjo, and a clarinet – these were the instruments. The trio took their places side by side, and began to play some rattling dance music, and beat time with their big boots.

It was getting very close to nine. Henry was standing in the door with his eyes directed up the road, his body swaying to the torture of his mental distress. He had been made to drink his wife's health and safety several times, and now Tom shouted: 'All hands stand by! One more drink, and she's here!'

Joe brought the glasses on a waiter, and served the party. I reached for one of the two remaining glasses, but Joe growled, under his breath: 'Drop that! Take the other.'

Which I did. Henry was served last. He had hardly swallowed his drink when the clock began to strike. He listened till it finished, his face growing pale and paler; then he said: 'Boys, I'm sick with fear. Help me – I want to lie down!' They helped him to the sofa. He began to nestle and drowse, but presently spoke like one talking in his sleep, and said: 'Did I hear horses' feet? Have they come?'

One of the veterans answered, close to his ear: 'It was Jimmy Parrish come to say the party got delayed, but they're right up the road a piece, and coming along. Her horse is lame, but she'll be here in half an hour.'

'Oh, I'm so thankful nothing has happened!'

He was asleep almost before the words were out of his mouth. In a moment those handy men had his clothes off, and had tucked him into his bed in the chamber where I had washed my hands. They closed the door and came back. Then they seemed preparing to leave, but I said: 'Please don't go, gentlemen. She won't know me; I am a stranger.'

They glanced at each other. Then Joe said: 'She? Poor thing, she's been dead nineteen years!'

'Dead?'

'That or worse. She went to see her folks half a year after she was married, and on her way back, on a Saturday evening, the Indians captured her within five miles of this place, and she's never been heard of since.'

'And he lost his mind in consequence?'

'Never has been sane an hour since. But he only gets bad when that time of the year comes round. Then we begin to drop in here, three days before she's due, to encourage him up, and ask if he's heard from her, and Saturday we all come and fix up the house with flowers, and get everything ready for a dance. We've done it every year for nineteen years. The first Saturday there was twenty-seven of us, without counting the girls; there's only three of us now, and the girls are all gone. We drug him to sleep, or he would go wild; then he's all right for another year – thinks she's with him till the last three or four days come round; then he begins to look for her, and gets out his poor old letter, and we come and ask him to read it to us. Lord, she was a darling!'